The Humbling of Meredith Martin

An Entertaining Edwardians novel

Patsy Trench

Book 5 in *Modern Women breaking the mould* series

© Prefab Publications

Published in 2024
by Prefab Publications, London

ISBN 978-0-9934537-9-3

'Early in life I had to choose between honest arrogance
and hypocritical humility. I chose the former and have
seen no reason to change.'

Frank Lloyd Wright

§

'Acting is all about honesty. If you can fake that, you've
got it made.'

George Burns

By the same author

NON-FICTION
Australia: a personal story series
The Worst Country in the World
A Country To Be Reckoned With
Australia and How To Find It

FICTION
Modern Women breaking the mould series
The Roaring Twenties
The Awakening of Claudia Faraday
The Purpose of Prudence de Vere
Entertaining Edwardians
The Makings of Violet Frogg
Mrs Morphett's Macaroons

All We Need Is Love (short stories)

§

As with my previous books *The Humbling of Meredith Martin* is a work of fiction that features one or two real people. While their lives and characters have been researched carefully their appearance in my novel is, needless to say, entirely invented.

Prologue Mrs Morphett's Macaroons

*The curtain rises on a warmly-lit stage. Two young
women, smartly dressed, stand centre stage gazing
winsomely out over the audience. Behind them, the
hint of a well-to-do drawing room painted onto
scenery. The orchestra starts up a familiar overture:
Oompah, oompah, oompah.*

MERRY & GAYE (sing)
>Two little gentle maids are we,
>Pert and wholesome as maids can be,
>Safe from the world's iniquity,
>Two little gentle maids.

GAYE
>One little maid begins to fret,
>>*(Orchestra: dadi dadi dadi dadi dadi dadida)*

MERRY
>Said, 'I've a brain, let's not forget.
>>*(dadi dadi dadi dadi dadi dadida)*

BOTH
>'I'm going to be a suffragette.'
>>*(dadi dadi dadi dadi dadi dadida)*
>Said two little gentle maids.

BOTH
> Two little maids who, all unwary,
> Joined a protest in Parli'ment Square-y,
> Now doing time in solitary –
> > *(pom-pom-pom-pom-pom-pom)*
> Two little maids in gaol,
> Two little maids in gaol.

> *Over the following the two women divest themselves*
> *of their outer garments to reveal prison dress,*
> *complete with arrows and apron. Meanwhile the*
> *lights change gradually, from the warm glow of their*
> *cosy drawing rooms to the harsh white light of a*
> *prison cell.*

GAYE
> Locked in a cell as cold as ice,

MERRY
> Sharing a bed with rats and mice,

BOTH
> No one paid such a heavy price
> As two little maids in gaol.
> > *(pom-pom-pom-pom-pom-pom)*

GAYE
> This little maid will soon be free,

MERRY
> This little maid as well, then we

BOTH
> 'll champion the cause tenaciously!
> Two little gentle maids!
> Two little gentle maids!

Two little maids, who all unwary,
Joined a protest in Parli'ment Square-y,
We're in to the death if necessary!
Two little gentle maids!
Two little gentle maids!

> *As the orchestra plays out the women fetch two
> banners from behind them declaring 'Votes for
> women!' and 'We will not be defeated!' Together they
> stand defiant, centre stage, as the song ends and the
> audience erupts.*

~

There is nothing, absolutely nothing on God's earth to compare with this moment.

Centre stage, before a packed audience of, what, several hundred at least, even in the compact space of the Touchstone Theatre, every eye upon you and every face alight and alert and utterly concentrated on the performance enacted on stage before them: you are a goddess. You can conquer the world. For one glorious moment you are a woman of immense power, you hold the universe in the palm of your hand. There is simply nothing like it.

Especially since, in the case of Meredith Martin, you not only rewrote the words to Gilbert and Sullivan's famous song yourself, you are performing it on stage thanks entirely to your own astounding ingenuity and downright cheek.

1: The cards

'Nothing,' said Mrs Vlatsky.

'What do you mean, nothing?' said Meredith.

'I am seeing nothing.' Mrs Vlatsky spread her hands apologetically. 'It happens.'

She flicked over a card, peered at it and shrugged. 'I'm sorry Mairie.'

'Never mind Mrs V, it's not your fault.'

Meredith slumped back in her chair and sighed heavily.

If you had told Meredith a few years ago that her day-to-day existence would be governed by a set of ordinary playing cards laid out in mysterious fashion by her landlady she would have laughed in your face. And yet there was no denying the cards had made the odd extraordinary predictions over the years, not least her success on stage at the Touchstone theatre in a play called *Mrs Morphett's Macaroons*.

She was working in a hat shop at the time, 'between acting engagements' as they say, the ultimate humiliation. She needed guidance and she looked to the cards to tell her what she should do. Mrs Vlatsky went through her usual ritual, and then she sat bolt upright in her chair and stared at the cards in some puzzlement.

'Well?' asked Meredith.

'They seem to be saying two things,' Mrs V pronounced, after a long moment.

'Which are?'

Mrs Vlatsky twitched. Her topknot was beginning to lurch sideways and she instinctively pushed it to the top of her head again. She looked at Merry with some excitement. 'They are saying you will succeed, and triumph.'

'Yes?'

'But only if you . . .' Mrs V gestured violently, 'do something – outside.'

'Outside what?'

'Not in the rules. That is what they are saying I believe.'

It was confusing, to say the least, but as Meredith interpreted it 'not in the rules' meant

that when she heard wind that a new theatre company was holding auditions for a play about suffragettes and she immediately applied to take part in them and heard nothing back, she took matters into her own hands and, encouraged by the cards, she gate-crashed them.

She was rewarded for her audacity by being given a role in the play along with her friend and sparring companion Gaye Worth. And though she said so herself together they brought the house down every night with their music hall turn in the smash hit *Mrs Morphett's Macaroons*.

It was how the theatre worked, was Meredith's view. A girl had to take chances, grab opportunities as and when she could, using guerrilla tactics where necessary. Meekness in the theatre did not inherit anything.

But that was several months ago now, since when both her working life and the cards – which even Meredith had to admit were closely linked, since she only felt a real need to consult them when her professional chips were down –

had been mystifyingly dormant.

'I don't understand how cards can say nothing,' she mumbled.

'It is a fallow time,' said her landlady. 'Fallow, is that the right word?'

'It certainly is.' Meredith drummed her fingers on the table top.

It was three years since Merry had arrived at Mrs Vlatsky's front door in Lambeth, clutching her possessions in one small suitcase. She had no recollection of how or why she ended up there, all she remembered was leaving her front door in St Leonard's Terrace and marching blindly down the street in no particular direction until several hours later she was standing outside a terraced house in Salamanca Road south of the river, which she did not remember crossing, staring at the 'Room to let' notice in the window and ringing Mrs Vlatsky's front doorbell.

Mrs V remembered the day well. It was a bitter November afternoon and the light was going as she answered the door to the tall and immaculately dressed young woman who stood on her doorstep clutching a small suitcase (French, she surmised, and extremely expensive) and said, 'I'm looking for a room.'

Now normally Mrs V would have invited the stranger into her front room, sat her down and offered tea and a chat, in the course of which she would have brought up the topic of references. But for some reason in this case all that seemed unnecessary, not to say inappropriate, and so she simply ushered the young lady up the stairs to the room on the first floor and left her to it.

When Mrs Vlatsky discovered in due course that her new lodger was an actress she had a momentary pang of doubt. She was not a theatregoer herself but she had the impression the people who worked in the theatrical profession were less than respectable. She need not have worried however. Meredith entertained no late-night visitors, male or female. In fact she received very few visitors at all, which in itself was a puzzle to Mrs Vlatsky because not only did she regard her lodger as one of the most striking women she had ever met, her breeding was unmistakable. And yet as time went on it became clear that matrimony, or even romance, were far from Meredith's mind. Her one and only concern, her 'passion' as she called it, was her career on the stage.

Then there was the business of her family.

'You are rifted from your family I believe,' said Mrs Vlatsky one day, completely out of the blue.

'"Rifted"?'

'A family estrangement, am I right?' Her landlady cocked her head to one side sympathetically.

Meredith did not reply.

'I thought so. Very sad, and very unnecessary.'

'What would you know about my family, Mrs Vlatsky?' Meredith snapped, though she did not mean to.

Mrs V looked momentarily flustered. 'Just a guess. The cards, they tell me many things.' She gestured vaguely at the offending sneaks, blandly laid out on the table before them, and shrugged.

How was Mrs Vlatsky to know about Meredith's family? Meredith certainly hadn't told her, she had not mentioned them ever since she arrived, indeed she did her best not to even think about them as the memory of her beloved parents, who had so firmly disowned her for choosing the stage as her profession, was a thorn in her side that only hurt when she allowed it to.

Other lodgers came and went. None of them stayed longer than a few months and Meredith had little to do with them. When she was absent from London for some months touring the provinces Mrs V kept her room open for her on her return, since when she had never even mentioned the payment of rent, and Meredith had coincidentally forgotten to remind her. She had assumed, conveniently perhaps, that her landlady was in receipt of some form of private income, and that, as Mrs V herself often remarked to her lodger with a warm smile, 'her company was all she required'.

And so the house on Salamanca Road in Lambeth became a kind of home for Meredith, and Mrs Vlatsky, with her cards and her topknot, her twinkling eyes and her mysterious insight, a kind of mother.

2: Gaye Worth

The theatre spawns unlikely acquaintances, and there was none more unlikely than the friendship between Meredith Martin and Gaye Worth.

They met at the Haymarket Theatre some years ago where they were appearing in a play together called *Johnson's Retribution,* directed by none other than the great Herbert Beerbohm Tree (arguably the West End's most celebrated actor-manager). They were playing rivals for the attention of the leading man, and in one scene when they were on stage together and during Meredith's longest and most passionate speech – which for reasons known only to herself she delivered direct to the audience – on realising that Gaye was pulling faces behind her back and producing titters from the auditorium, once the scene was over and they were offstage she socked her in the jaw.

Summoned to explain themselves to the management the two actresses fell into a kind of impromptu double act and, so successful were they at running rings around the management they not only managed to avoid being sacked, they decided once the run of the play was over to develop the act, calling themselves 'Merry and Gaye'. They performed largely improvised sketches and songs in private living rooms (with some success) and on the streets of the West End (with less success), finally reaching their zenith in *Mrs Morphett's Macaroons*.

Meredith both admired and resented her fellow performer. Gaye had been born, as she was wont to claim, in a trunk in a dressing room between shows at the music hall her parents were appearing in (an exaggeration, but only just). She made her first professional stage appearance at the age of five, and bullied and chivvied by her father she had continued to perform in music hall and in straight theatre ever since almost without a break.

That Gaye was able to step outside her character on stage sufficiently in order to deliberately make other people laugh showed her to be a real trouper, in Meredith's eyes. It took years of experience and a good deal of sophistication to carry it off. It was admirable, in a sense, and Merry secretly envied her.

At the same time she resented the fact that Gaye had things so easy. She had never had to run the gauntlet of disreputable agents and managers who vanished from theatres at the end of a run without paying the actors. Or endured lengthy tours in god-forsaken towns in obscure parts of the country for so little pay the actors had to beg, borrow or steal their costumes and hitch lifts between engagements. Most importantly of all Gaye had not been turned out of the family home for following her dream, quite the opposite. She even had the gall to claim she found the whole performing business tedious and only kept at it because she didn't know what else to do. It was sickening.

Yet here they were, the ebony-haired, six-feet-in-her-stockings brigadier's daughter and the five-foot-nothing blonde daughter of a cockney music hall comedian, huddled together in a gloomy corner of the dingy Primrose Inn, a little-known establishment tucked away down a forgettable side street off the Strand; the doors of which Meredith had on more than occasion vowed she would never darken, not least because it was a haven for out of work actors who thanks to the forbearance of the *patron* were allowed to spend whole evenings or afternoons sitting over a single pint of light ale or lemonade (or a mixture of both) publicly bemoaning the wretchedness of their profession.

'God, this place is depressing,' she pronounced, by way of making her point.

'Cheer up. It's better than sitting home alone, ain't it?'

Meredith grunted.

'There's some interesting people here, if you could be bothered to find out.'

'I'll take your word for it.'

Meredith sipped her whisky sour and gazed moodily about her.

'You know your trouble?' said Gaye.

'No, do tell me,' said Meredith.

'You're a snob.'

'Am I indeed. If by a 'snob' you mean I have standards then yes, I am proud to be a snob.'

'"Standards"? What are they when they're at home?' Gaye took a long swig of her brown ale.

'I don't know how you can drink that stuff,' said Meredith.

'There, see what I mean?' Gaye took another swig and smacked her lips in a manner that was deliberately vulgar. 'It pays to get on with people in this business you know. It's what it's all about if you think about it.'

'I do get on with people, some people. I just don't see why one should have to . . .' she stopped.

'You was going to say "lower yourself", wasn't you? I can tell. I know what you're going to say before you say it.'

'Well, clever you.'

'Something'll turn up. Something always does.'

'For you maybe.'

There was a pause. Gaye studied her friend for a moment.

'You just want to be a leading lady, don't you?'

'What's wrong with that? Doesn't everyone? Don't you?'

'Me? No, not really. And your trouble is you behave like one. It's all very well if you're famous, and I mean really famous, like whatshername Ellen Terry, or that Mrs Patrick Campbell, that's when you can behave all hoity-toity. Not that I'm saying that's what they do, but if they did, they could get away with it. Your trouble is,' she took another swig, 'you think you're a leading lady and you ain't. Aren't.'

It hadn't occurred to Meredith before but she rather fancied Gaye very deliberately became more of a cockney when it was just the two of them than when they were in company, just to be annoying.

'I can't see what's wrong with ambition,' she said. 'I've done my time, I've slummed it in the provinces, I've appeared in the West End, twice.'

Gaye did so. 'So?'

'I will never understand,' Meredith leaned across the table almost aggressively. 'How one can be the toast of the town one moment and invisible the next.'

'It's how it works ducky.'

'So how is one supposed to progress in this business? What is one expected to do?'

'Keep going. Or not. It's up to you.'

Meredith leaned back and gave her friend a wan smile.

'We were a good double-act, weren't we?' she said.

'We was the best.'

'The Duchess and the Cockney.'

'"Two little gentle maids are we."'

'Merry and Gaye.'

'Gave yourself top billing, as per.'

There was a pause. Meredith toyed with her glass.

'Would you ever . . .' she began.

'Not on your life.' Gaye shook her head violently and her curls wobbled. 'I've got other plans.'

'Oh, and what are they?'

'If you really want to know I'm giving up the business. I'm getting married.'

There was a silence. Merry sighed, and turned to look blankly out of the window.

'Well, aren't you going to congratulate me?'

'If you really want me to.' She shifted her gaze to the far side of the room. 'I don't understand why getting married means you have to quit the profession.'

'I don't have to.'

'He's telling you what to do already, is he? Before you're even married?'

'Nope, I made up my own mind all on my ownsome. I'm going to have babies. Lots of them.'

'Bully for you.'

'And I get to leave home,' added Gaye, with a twinkle.

She went on to regale her friend, unprompted, with the life story and detailed description of her intended: what he did (a carpenter cum set painter), where they met (at the Alexandra Music Hall where she'd been working as her father's skivvy in return for her keep), the colour of his hair (light brown with hints of red), his cheeky sense of humour, which is what really did for her in the end, she giggled. He had Big Ambitions, she went on without pausing for breath, he was going to get out of the entertainment world altogether and go into Speculation, whatever that was. He was going to start up his own business and make so much money she would never need to work again and she could live like a pig in clover and have as many babies as she wanted.

It sounded like hell on earth to Meredith but even she had the wit to hold her tongue on occasion. As she listened to her friend burbling on she marvelled at what happened to people in love that turned them into such blithering idiots. Shakespeare was right, it was a form of madness.

She also felt something else, less easily definable. She felt abandoned, and inexplicably betrayed. While Meredith liked to imagine she was quite self-reliant she acknowledged her occasional meetings with her friend, her best and to be truthful her only friend, were an important part of her life. Granted it meant putting up with her insults, not to mention her home truths, as nobody knew Merry better than Gaye. But in a world where *nobody* said what they meant Gaye's outspokenness came as a blast of fresh air, or a douche of cold water, depending on how one looked at it.

She was tempted to tell Gaye about the cards but she was afraid she would be laughed at. Or perhaps that Gaye might want to have hers read, which would reveal to her the disasters that lay ahead; or worse, that they would spell out infinite happiness amid endless featherbeds of babies.

The few hours spent in the grimness of the Primrose were not wasted however, as thanks to a tip-off from an acquaintance of Gaye's – 'See? It don't matter what you know so much as who you get to talk to,' she proclaimed – Merry found herself later in the year once again on tour; this time under a Top Management visiting Number One theatres in Major Cities only, playing the (non-leading) role of Miss Mabel Chiltern in Oscar Wilde's *An Ideal*

Husband: a silly little thing who spends most of the play flirting with the languorously idle Lord Goring and then, to the surprise of absolutely nobody, marrying him. It was a vacuous role in an equally vacuous play and Mabel was not a good fit for Merry. However her Lord Goring was at least as tall as she was and they continued their onstage flirtation offstage, to some extent; until Merry came to the conclusion that he batted for the other side, as they say. Which made everything that much more fun and a good deal safer.

3: Here comes the bride

The wedding party was a jolly affair held in the Crown and Anchor pub just a hop and a skip from the Alexandra Music Hall in Shoreditch, where the bride and the groom had first met. The bride looked as if she'd stepped straight off the top of a wedding cake: layer upon layer of white lace billowed over acres of petticoats, and in the midst of it all her tiny pink face peeked out, flushed with sheer joy and happiness.

The bridegroom was every bit a match for her in a midnight blue two-piece with yellow waistcoat and orange bow tie that *twirled*. Merry thought she was imagining it until he demonstrated it to her in close up. He was almost exactly the same height as the bride, with a shock of orange hair – he'd dyed it to match his tie, he told her – and the bawdiest sense of humour north of Spitalfields. He told outrageously *outré* jokes accompanied by a broad grin and a twirl of the bow tie, but in such a way as to disarm the most severe of matrons.

They danced – oh, how they danced! To the accompaniment of a band comprising mouth organ, concertina, violin and drum they whirled around the room in a bizarre medley of tango, Viennese waltz and gallop. At one point Gaye's father, never one to miss an opportunity to upstage his daughter, took to the dance floor with his wife and proceeded to perform a routine, part tap, part soft-shoe shuffle. Then in a moment to stop the hardest of hearts, their daughter Gaye joined in, and together they recreated, with a deftness and a precision that took even Meredith's breath away, an act they had first performed, so they told the assembly, when Gaye was just ten years old.

Meredith had never visited a music hall. It was not the sort of place a young lady ventured into unaccompanied. Yet as she looked on at the sheer merriment and exuberance she began to see its appeal. It was joyous, it was riotous, it was loud and raucous and uninhibited – everything a brigadier's daughter with aspirations to play Shakespeare had been brought up to disparage.

'Come on, Miss Martin!' Somebody grabbed her hand and before she could resist she was being pulled onto the makeshift dance floor and forced to join a line of dancers performing their own version of a knees-up. Arms around one another's waists, as the music grew louder so she recognised a kind of song – not easily identifiable as people were singing different verses of it at the same time – "Don't dilly-dally on the way". To her annoyance she realised she was probably the only person in the room who did not know the words. But she joined in, and sang louder if more out of tune than anyone (Meredith was not a singer), but nobody minded. And she thought, not for the first time, how much more fun it was being *working class*. Not caring a hoot about anything except having a good time.

Fun, the sheer, unadulterated sort, had not featured much in Meredith's life. There was taste to be taken account of, and propriety, not to mention restraint and appropriateness. She felt almost sorry for herself.

When the music finally stopped and the dancers

dispersed, exhausted, hanging onto one another to stop themselves from falling over, Billy took to the floor to deliver his version of a wedding speech. He described Gaye as his 'little peach – round and soft on the outside and juicy underneath', which drew raucous laughter from the assembled guests. He described in his own way how they first met, how 'she weren't much to look at so I didn't take much notice till she tripped up the stairs once and showed me her legs,' at which point his blushing, giggling (and slightly inebriated) bride stood up and threw a spoon at him. He called her his little darlin' and 'the sweetest natured little thing I ever did see, and so what if she was on the plump side, she'll be twice the size in no time once I've got a hold of her.' He talked about all the babies they were going to have, and the pretty little house he was going to buy for her, with a garden in the front and a garden at the back with roses and a little fence running around it to keep the little nippers from running out into the road. At this point Merry spotted the tears running down Gaye's cheek, and she even had to blink to stop her own eyes watering.

When he was done Gaye's father stood up and, thumbs tucked into his waistcoat, he strolled to the centre of the room and turned to glower at the each member of the assembly in turn. He stood there for some time, like a prize fighter waiting for a challenge, and Merry saw a look of something approaching fear cross Gaye's face.

She knew about Gaye's relationship with her father. He was known to be something of a tyrant when it came to his younger daughter, especially regarding her professional life. There was never any question as to the direction it would take, it was all set out for her. Gaye had first appeared on stage, with her mother and elder sister, at the age of five, and it had gone on from there. Education, such as it was, took place in the nature of song and dance lessons taught by her parents. Father made sure Gaye and her sister were in constant work throughout their childhood, whether they liked it or not, and as soon as she was of age he insisted his daughter pay him rent, and between engagements he had her working for him in lieu (so unlike dear Mrs Vlatsky, thought Meredith).

He was still glaring around the room. He certainly knew how to hold an audience, Merry had to grudgingly admit. He was waiting for complete silence, for the chatter and the clatter to cease and for the full and undivided attention of every person in the room to be focused on him. Finally, as the guests settled and the place grew quiet enough that you could hear the plop of the proverbial pin, he began to sing, at first softly:

    'There is a flower within my heart,
    Daisy, Daisy.
    Planted one day by a glancing dart,
    Planted by Daisy Bell.
    Whether she loves me or loves me not,
    Sometimes it's hard to tell,
    Yet I am longing to share the lot,
    A beautiful Daisy Bell.'

Then with a flourish he reached out a hand towards his daughter, and without a break in the song, as she got to her feet and took his hand . . .

    'Daisy, daisy, give me your answer, do.
    I'm half crazy, all for the likes of you.
    It wasn't a stylish marriage,
    He can't afford a carriage,'

She joined in with the song, hand in hand with her father, swaying together.

    'But you look sweet
    Upon the seat

Of a bicycle built for two.'

Then he took hold of her and began to whirl her around the room in a waltz. At which point, without prompting, the crowd began to sing, Meredith along with them.

'Daisy, daisy, give me your answer, do . . .'

They sang like the professionals they were, in four-part harmony. Merry did her best with the words, and kept her unmusical voice quiet.

'I'm half crazy, all for the likes of you.

It won't be a stylish marriage,

He can't afford a carriage,.

But you'll look sweet

Upon the seat

Of a bicycle built for two.'

On it went, verse chorus verse, they knew it by heart, of course they did. The song got louder, the harmony more arbitrary. Meredith found herself weeping openly, as she'd never done before. She wept for Gaye's happiness, she wept for the loss of her own parents, she wept for the realisation that when a person gets married they pretty well disappear from the scene, and that her on-off love-hate friendship with Gaye Worth, now Tillings, would never be quite the same again.

4: Meredith's mother

How odd it is, mused Meredith's mother to herself, that while it is considered respectable, not to say *de rigueur*, to attend the theatre, and more specifically to be *seen* to attend the theatre, should one's offspring have the gall to choose to make it their profession they risked being disowned altogether.

She was watching the two men, her husband and the husband of the woman who stood beside her (chatting about hats), talking animatedly to one another. It was the interval of a play at the Comedy Theatre and of one thing she was sure, they were not talking about the play.

Theatre audiences were strange creatures, she thought. Most of them were there to be seen rather than to see, or to pass the time between drinks and a late-night supper at the Cavendish or some such. Some had come to watch the leading actor and actress, as the star system was still alive and kicking in the first decade of the twentieth century. Her companion, whose name was Susanna, was there for purely social reasons, and the husband she'd dragged along with her only tolerated the experience to appease her, and for the chance of a hearty conversation in the interval with the husband of his wife's friend, a man of strong opinions and a robust sense of humour.

A more forthright woman, or perhaps a braver one,

would have stood up to her husband when he ordered Meredith from the house all those years ago. But Mrs Stephenson was neither particularly forthright nor brave. Besides, she was married to a brigadier. And when a brigadier makes a decision he never goes back on it, even if he realises immediately that it is the wrong decision.

Virginia Stephenson was at heart a conservative woman with conservative values. She loved her husband. She loved his certainty, the black and white geometrical clarity of his world. By contrast hers was a swirl of changing colours and moving shapes, where very little was certain or fixed; except perhaps her love of the arts and the drama in particular. She felt largely responsible for her daughter's choice of career as it was she who had introduced her to the theatre in the first place, as a result of which Meredith had developed a remarkable talent for mimicry which she was wont to display at the drop of a hat to visiting guests at St Leonard's Terrace. It was inevitable that before long one or more of them would declare she should go on the stage; which – after a few months of 'training' at the School for Elocution run by a one-time actor by the name of Willard Featherbridge – she did.

Once Meredith's parents had come to the conclusion that their daughter's ambition was serious and she was not just dabbling in the business, they – or rather the brigadier – delivered his ultimatum: give it up or leave. And to the astonishment of both parents and the secret dismay of her mother, Meredith did the latter.

That was now three years ago and they had heard nothing from Meredith since. Virginia fretted, and her husband knew she fretted, and he was sympathetic up to a point as he adored his wife. But nothing would make him change his mind and his wife knew better than to bring up the subject. Meredith's name was never even mentioned. It was as if she had never existed.

So a year ago when Virginia spotted a poster on a wall in a street off Sloane Square advertising *Mrs Morphett's Macaroons*, featuring her very own daughter under her stage name of Meredith Martin, she immediately booked herself a single ticket to the first night at the Touchstone Theatre. She attended it alone, with neither her husband's nor her daughter's knowledge, on the pretext of visiting her club. It was the first lie she had ever told her husband, but it was not the last.

She had admitted as much to her friend Susanna Gulliver, the very woman she stood next to now. She had badly needed to confide in somebody, and it was perhaps fortuitous that among all her many friends Virginia should choose that particular lady. Mrs Gulliver was known as 'a fixer', the sort of practical, no-nonsense woman who had an immediate solution to any problem. This entailed a certain ruthlessness at times, such as when she locked her own son in his bedroom for forty-eight hours, without food or water, for swearing at her.

Mrs Gulliver had an immediate answer: put a private detective onto her.

'What's a private detective?'

'A spy. I've done it more than once when I thought Henry was up to no good. I know just the person. He's retired from the Metropolitan Police, he's as dogged as a – as a dog. And discreet. To the point of dullness. But who cares about dullness? He is utterly reliable, I couldn't recommend him highly enough.'

Mrs Stephenson hesitated. 'You're suggesting I hire a total stranger to spy on my daughter?'

'At least you will know what she's up to, whom she sees, where she goes. He can follow her when she leaves the theatre at night back to wherever it is she is living. And once you have her address you can confront her as you see fit, if you see fit. Without . . .' Susanna paused for a wry smile, 'your husband even knowing.'

This naturally was several steps too far for Meredith's mother. But once again her hesitancy was her downfall, or maybe it was her saviour, for before she had time to open her mouth to object her friend was scribbling a note and handing it to her maid, 'To be delivered immediately please'.

And so it was that, in a remarkably short time, retired Inspector Lucas, ex Scotland Yard, had been able to report back to Meredith's mother the precise address where her daughter was living at Number 15 Salamanca Road in Lambeth.

She had waited a week. She couldn't really say why, again it was the uncertainty, and of course the deception. But then the uncertainty of not knowing how her daughter was, whether she was happy in her chosen profession, whether or not she had a 'beau', or even a husband, was overpowering. Which is why Mrs Stephenson found herself one evening when she knew her daughter was at the theatre knocking on the door of No 15 Salamanca Road and being greeted by a stout, middle-aged woman wearing a hat, who peered nervously into the darkness and said: 'Yes?'

'I am so sorry to bother you,' said Mrs Stephenson, and she introduced herself.

'Come in, come in!' cried Mrs Vlatsky, as she stepped aside and ushered her unexpected guest into her front room. 'This is such a surprise! Sit down, please, sit down! Mairy is not here, she is at the theatre, but she should be back, well . . .' Mrs V glanced at the clock, 'perhaps not for an hour or two. May I offer you some tea? My name is

Vlatsky, Katarina Vlatsky.'

Mrs Stephenson smiled and shook her head as she took a seat opposite Mrs Vlatsky. In the light of Mrs V's front room she realised the lady's hat was not a hat but her own hair piled in a kind of makeshift bun on top of her head, and which was, distractingly, lurching drunkenly to one side.

She explained, briefly, her reason for the visit, which was not to see her daughter but rather to find out how she was. She described the background circumstances, as much as was necessary, and she finished with, 'Do you think she is happy?'

'Oh yes,' said Mrs. 'Now she is. Vairy happy. She loves to be playing.'

'Playing?'

'In the theatre. It is what she loves most of all. And in the West End!' Mrs V clapped her hands together like a child. 'She is the toast of the town! Is that the true expression?' She leaned anxiously across to Mrs Stephenson and absent-mindedly shoved her topknot back to the top of her head. 'It is what she tells me.'

'That is very good to hear,' said Meredith's mother.

She went on to quiz Mrs Vlatsky, as gently as she could, on how long Meredith had been staying there, what she had been doing over the years, what her plans were for the future, if she had any, and did she . . . And here Virginia hesitated as it seemed she was, perversely perhaps, crossing some kind of a line . . . Did she appear to have a special male friend?

Mrs Vlatsky laughed heartily at this. 'No! I tell her – I say you should have a lover, a beautiful young woman like you. You should be married! But no.' She sighed dramatically. 'I cannot persuade her, not even with the cards. She is not interested, she tells me. She only wants to be on stage. Nothing else is a matter to her, nothing. Her mood is up,' she gestured, 'and down, when she is not working.'

'You read cards?'

'Yes,' said Mrs Vlatsky, with a slight shrug of apology. 'Would you like me . . .?'

'Oh – no, thank you. How – er – interesting.'

There was a short pause.

'Can I ask you,' said Virginia, 'how my daughter is managing for money?'

'Money!' Mrs V made a helpless gesture. 'She is terrible! Terrible with money! She earns it she spends it!' she shook her head violently and her topknot almost came apart completely. 'She does not save, she told me. She feels she does not need to save because she thinks she will always be working. She thinks she will be soon a leading lady, with so much money she does not know what to do. "And then, Mrs Vlatsky," she tells to me, "I will pay you back all the rent I did not pay when I did not work, many times over!"' And again she hooted with laughter.

Virginia reached into her bag and drew out an envelope. She placed it on the table in front of Mrs Vlatsky and kept her hand upon it.

'Please take this,' she said.

Mrs V recoiled, as if she had been presented with a snake.

'Please, I insist. This is for her rent, when she is unable to pay it, and a little bit over.' She withdrew her hand. 'I have also written down my address. And what I would like you to do, if you would be so kind, I would like you to write to me, every so often, when you can, and tell me how she is.'

There was a long silence as Mrs V continued to stare at the envelope in a kind of terror.

'Can I ask you to do that for me, please?'

To her shame Meredith's mother felt a tear emerge from the corner of her eye and escape down her cheek before she could reach for a handkerchief.

'I don't want to see her. Or rather,' she dabbed at her eye, 'I realise that would not be – possible, or appropriate. But I do want to know how she is. I would be so grateful.'

And now Mrs V was crying too, more openly and much more noisily. She too pulled out a handkerchief and blew into it, loudly.

Meredith's mother got to her feet. 'Thank you for everything you have done for her, Mrs Vlatsky,' she said. 'Thank you for being . . . for being her mother.' She laughed, briefly, and with embarrassment.

And before Mrs V had time to reply, or to object, she left.

All that had taken place the previous year, since which time Mrs Vlatsky had conscientiously written once a month, not always with much information. Meredith had been absent on a tour for some months, she wrote, and of course she had kept her room free for her. And she admitted at that very moment Meredith appeared in low spirits, although she was sure that would change, and soon, the moment she found herself a new engagement.

It was not much comfort, but it was better than nothing.

5: The Lambeth walk

The days were long, and empty, when Merry was not working. She rose late and spent the morning and sometimes the afternoon too just wandering around the local vicinity. Her landlady's generosity, while it meant she did not feel compelled to find alternative employment in these lean times, hardly covered any form of entertainment in the shape of visits to restaurants or nights out. So it was a struggle to find ways to fill the day.

You would not guess, were you to see her strolling the streets of Lambeth, that she was anything other than a smart young lady going about her business. She walked with what appeared to be supreme confidence and a kind of natural superiority that made fellow strollers automatically move out of her way. Tall, statuesque and impeccably dressed, she was every bit the brigadier's daughter. And to top it all, literally and figuratively, she wore spectacular hats.

The hats were genuine masterpieces of design and engineering and Meredith was the proud owner of no fewer than three of them: each one unique, and of course handmade, and filched from the shelves of Mme Poulesse's milliner's shop for the moneyed and exclusive – where as aforesaid Meredith had once worked as Madame's assistant.

They (the hats) stood Merry in good stead. No one, especially in the theatre business, wants to be associated with anyone who appears to be down on their luck. The hats announced to the world that Meredith was a well-to-do young professional woman whose life was in perfect order.

Look a little closer however and one might spot the odd frayed cuff and threadbare patch on an outfit that, as the saying goes, 'had seen better days'. Had in fact seen almost every day in the last month or so ever since Meredith's life began to take what she regarded as a downward turn.

In the early days, when she first moved – or was removed – from the rose-gardened, servanted affluence across the river to the grey and dubious drabness of south London, Meredith had spent as little time on the streets of Lambeth as she possibly could. She strode directly from her front door to the nearest 'bus or tram stop, and from the safety of her chosen transport she could look down on the ugly streets of her new neighbourhood with comparative safety, protected from the smells of the tanneries and faulty drains and the raucous cries of costermongers, not to mention the pickpockets. For Meredith was, as anyone could see, a fish out of water in Lambeth: a lady who had by dint of fortune fetched up in a slum.

Over time however she had become used to her surroundings so she was no longer aware of the stink and she knew which alleyways to avoid. She walked, or indeed strode, with straight back and eyes fixed firmly ahead, and with purpose, even if in reality she had none. In days past, when she had a bob or two, she would make for Lambeth Pier and jump on a steamboat for the one penny ride to Tower Bridge. Or she'd kill time weaving her way through the washing lines to the street markets in Lambeth Walk, just for the noise and the colour and the diversion. On occasion she would take a detour to the Canterbury Music Hall near Westminster Bridge, where she would scrutinise the bills for a familiar name among the acts currently appearing there. She even became almost friendly with the stage doorkeeper, whose name she learned was Al, and who, so he claimed, could 'get her the best seat in the house' in return for some unspecified service which Meredith did not stop long enough to discuss.

It would have been more fun to have spent the time with a 'chum'. But as her friend had told her only too plainly Meredith wasn't good at chums. Her haughty manner, a product of her upbringing and which despite the family rift she continued to nurture, did not endear her to her fellow actors. The nearest she had come to a genuine friendship had been with Gaye Worth. (She was partly looking for Gaye's name on the bills outside the Canterbury.) And as predicted now she was Mrs Tillings she had effectively vanished off the face of the earth.

On this particular day in February, the bleakest, most wretched month of the year, Meredith found herself heading along Lambeth Road to the Embankment, where she stopped to watch the activity on the river; an occupation she found both diverting and depressing, as there is nothing worse when one is feeling down on one's luck than watching other people going about their business as if they had not a care in the world.

She took the steps up to the bridge and walked to a halfway point on the river, that great divide between the opulence and familiarity of her childhood to the north and her current shabby existence to the south. Her past and her present. As she did so she idly wondered, were she to throw herself in (the thought had crossed her mind, if it weren't for what she might swallow on the way down), which side of the river her body would wash up on.

35

6: The Court Theatre

She read about the play in *The Stage*, and while normally even in her current straitened circumstances Merry would never have dreamed of putting herself forward as a 'woman in the crowd' at a suffragette rally, it was a way out of her current decline and an opportunity to appear at the Court Theatre.

It was a known fact in the acting profession that if one wanted to enhance one's reputation as a serious actor the Court was The Place To Be. It was not because of the money; the current regime not only paid worse than any West End theatre, they paid every actor *the same*, whether she were a leading lady or a member of the crowd. It was because the Court was known as the 'thinking person's theatre', where intelligent audiences could experience thought-provoking works by Henrik Ibsen and George Bernard Shaw; where the acting was said to be in a different league to other theatres, thanks to 'a directing intelligence' which paid attention to every part in the play, no matter how small.

This directing intelligence was a young man called Granville Barker, who with his business partner John Vedrenne had established a new kind of theatre in Sloane Square whose aim was to make art rather than money (a quaint idea at the time), where the playwright was king (ditto), with a company of actors performing in new plays that challenged the status quo.

It was this reputation, along with encouragement from the cards – 'Seize the opportunity!' cried Mrs Vlatsky, without indicating what the opportunity might be – that persuaded Meredith to uncharacteristically agree to play a tiny part in *Votes for Women*, a new play written by an American actress called Elizabeth Robins.

The play featured a woman called Vida Levering, who spent her days espousing the cause of women's rights and helping the homeless, but whose real motivation was to persuade an ex lover and ambitious Member of Parliament, whose child she had carried and been persuaded to abort many years ago, to sign a paper in support of women's right to vote by way of retribution.

Now Meredith knew a certain amount about the suffragettes, thanks to *Mrs Morphett's Macaroons*. However it would be true to say that secretly she had very little time for the presumptuous, strident types who stalked the streets with banners shouting 'Votes for Women'. She had not herself seen any of them but she had heard of these people who thought they had the right to march *en masse* along London's busiest streets, causing huge traffic jams, and all in the cause of granting women the vote. She really couldn't see the point of it all, and as for ending up in gaol for 'causing a public nuisance', well, what did that achieve? Personally speaking she found it perfectly possible to make her own way in life, in her own style, without the necessity of voting.

But nobody needed to know any of that. At least she was working again, albeit playing an unnamed, anonymous woman in the crowd for a number of matinées of a play directed by London theatre's new young Turk.

Rehearsals were eye-opening. Meredith was used to

being told when to stand or sit, where and when to move –
instructions she often ignored anyway – and that was it.
But Barker's approach was utterly different. He began by
seating his actors in a circle and talking to them about the
play, about his working methods and what as a company
he hoped to achieve. How it was not his position to tell
them what to do or how to deliver a line, he explained
with a smile. His responsibility was simply to ensure they
were travelling along the same tramlines together, with
the same spirit and energy. The Play, he stressed, was
Everything.

He was an actor himself of course, which explained
part of it, and a playwright. He was also extraordinarily
young, and distractingly handsome, with sleek black hair
parted meticulously in the centre and a gentle, humorous
manner. Even Merry was disarmed.

He then went around the circle inviting each person in
turn to talk about the play from their character's point of
view. Meredith listened abstractedly, trying but mostly
failing to take her eyes off the young man in charge, who
was listening intently as each actor discussed their
characters as if they knew them intimately, which of
course they did. After a while she switched her attention
to the leading lady, Edith Wynne Matthison, who was
playing Vida Levering, and pondered on her constitution.

It had been drummed into Meredith's consciousness in
the course of her career that until she became an
established leading actress herself, in order to get ahead of
her rivals she should learn the lines of the leading lady of
any play she was appearing in so that, in the event of the
lady's demise and in the absence of an official understudy
she could step immediately into her shoes. Miss Wynne
Matthison looked depressingly healthy, and while the play
was scheduled for a few performances only the Court did

not run to understudies, so Meredith felt it was nothing less than her duty to study her every move, because you never know your luck.

But then it was her turn to speak and so she gave a slightly nervous laugh and muttered she was simply a 'woman in the crowd' at a suffragette rally and really, she had little idea who she was or whether it mattered. Unlike most if not all her fellow actors she had not read the play, not all the way through. She had glanced at her lines – she only appeared in the second act – and that was about it. But that was not enough for Granville Barker.

'Everyone,' he said, addressing the entire company, 'in my plays is important, equally so. As they are in life.'

'Oh.' Meredith cleared her throat. 'Well then. She – I – have two lines. "Hear hear" and "let her speak".'

'Yes?'

'So I imagine,' she went on, 'I am not a suffragette as such. But obviously I am in support of the cause.'

'And who are you?'

'My name is Meredith Martin, I'm . . .'

'Is that the name of your character?'

'Oh, I see what you mean. No. Well, let's say I was passing by, on my way to – somewhere or other – and I stopped to listen to the speakers.'

'And were you already a supporter of women's suffrage, or is this the first time you have encountered it?'

'I think . . .' she thought frantically, 'I was aware of it, but I'd never given it much proper thought before. I am – a secretary in the, er, Ministry of Home Affairs, I'm very busy, I have responsibilities, but now and again – it is very much a man's world, Home Affairs, and sometimes I find myself being patronised, treated like an underling, a sort of decorative trinket they can use or discard as they see fit. Whereas I am in fact a highly intelligent woman.'

Barker nodded appreciatively. 'And were you to be given the vote do you suppose your superiors might treat you with the respect you deserve?'

'It's worth a try,' she tilted her head in a manner she supposed coquettish.

'And might you, as a result of listening to the speakers, decide to take up the cause?'

'It depends on them I suppose, how persuasive they are.' She turned to smile at the assembled company and one or two smiled back.

'Excellent answer,' said Barker. 'I look forward to hearing your decision in due course.'

She flushed. She had to admit that it was remarkable how, with a little gentle questioning, he had helped to turn her tiny character with her two tiny lines into a fully-fleshed person, a senior secretary in the Home Office, holder of secrets and responsibilities. She spent the following moments imagining the kind of surroundings a senior secretary might find herself in, the view from her window, of Whitehall probably, although come to think of it she had no idea where the Home Office was; and pondering on what sort of costume a high-ranking professional woman might wear – something French, possibly, or was that not unpatriotic? – no matter, the pinched waist was essential (she had better lay off Mrs V's cupcakes for the duration). In between musings she cocked half an ear to Mr Barker as he continued around the circle, encouraging, probing, urging each actor one by one to flesh out their characters with names, professions, backgrounds and prejudices, until bit by bit a recognisable person emerged.

'Excellent,' said the good man finally. 'And let us bear in mind that none of this is set in stone. As in the case of Miss Martin ('He remembers my name!' Merry gasped to herself) your minds are not necessarily yet firmly made up. You are attending the rally to be convinced, or otherwise, and it is up to the various speakers to convince you.'

It was quite thrilling. It was almost like real life.

When the time came to put the second act of the play on its feet Meredith found herself in the company of a young man with unruly hair and a chirpy manner, whose name was Freddy. He told her it was not the first time he'd worked at the Court for Barker, he was what you might call a regular company member, he'd even played the lead in a Shaw play recently. This piece of news surprised Meredith and she privately wondered what it was he had done to reduce him from leading actor to supernumerary.

She introduced herself as Miss Magdalena Makepiece – 'with an "i"' – personal secretary to the Minister for Home Affairs. In the intervening days since the first rehearsal Miss Makepiece had become more than a character drawn randomly from the air, she was Meredith's *alter ego*, the person she might have been had the lure of the theatre not grabbed her, occupying a senior position in the Ministry and living in opulent premises in, let's say, the Albany. With a balcony overlooking the river. Yet frustrated by her lack of advancement, which is why she had paused on her way back to the office to listen to the young women and men addressing the crowd from a platform in Trafalgar Square.

Freddy cheerfully announced he was a builder's labourer on his way home from work who'd been drawn into the Square by the crowd and spent the time heckling. He also had only two lines - "What do you know about it? You can't even talk grammar," and "Three cheers for the dumb lady!" Which naturally led to a healthy and increasingly heated argument between them. With each rehearsal so their characters varied and grew and changed, so one day Meredith was the owner of a brothel and Freddy the boss of a gang of boy chimney sweeps, then the wife of a diplomat and a postman who was secretly spying on behalf of the government. On one occasion they even swopped lines and characters, and if Mr Barker noticed, which he undoubtedly did, he did not complain. They had the best fun in the world and were even more encouraged when Barker, working his way slowly around the rehearsal space, eavesdropped on their conversation and nodded approvingly.

7: Rehearsals

Meredith attended every rehearsal, even when she was not called. She sat at the edge of the rehearsal room, observing the leading lady keenly, as she had promised herself, and with increasing curiosity as she began to recognise she was watching an actress at the top of her game.

Edith Wynne Matthison was not a natural beauty. She was not a woman you would turn to look at in the street. There was very little remarkable about her, and it was surprising, in Meredith's view, that she had got as far as she had in the theatre profession.

But the more she watched the more she marvelled. Vida Levering was not an easy character to portray: an idealistic, self-sacrificing martyr who as a result of a personal tragedy had devoted her life to helping others, in particular homeless women and the suffragette movement. By far the most intelligent character in the play, prone to quiet put-downs and patronising asides, she was not an easy person to like.

Yet without changing a word of the text between them Miss Wynne Matthison and her mentor and guide Granville Barker transformed Miss Levering into a fallible, occasionally faltering, layered and sympathetic human being, often by playing against the line. So what on the page appeared to be a superior put-down was delivered self-deprecatingly, almost apologetically. When it came to her passionate speeches, of which there were quite a few – some addressed to the crowds in Trafalgar Square in Act 2 and some to her erstwhile lover and father of her aborted child Geoffrey Stoner – she did something quite unexpected: she lowered her voice. She spoke quietly and plainly, with great restraint, without side and without gesture, and the effect was electrifying. As an object lesson in suppressed emotion it was without parallel.

But it was not how Meredith saw the role, not at all. Passionate speeches lent themselves to passionate delivery, which Meredith excelled in. She was proud to claim she was the only actress whose voice according to none other than Herbert Beerbohm Tree was able to reach the far corners of the theatre without effort. That Miss Wynne Matthison and Barker should choose to go quite in the opposite direction was frankly counter-intuitive. And yet, as Meredith was forced to acknowledge, it worked.

Occasionally Barker would gently interrupt, usually to say 'Do less'. Under his gentle coaxing his leading lady became less of an actress and more of a complex yet sympathetic human being. So remarkable was it that Meredith quite forgot she was there to study the woman's performance in detail in order to step in if and when necessary. She began to realise, to her considerable dismay, how superior, how very far above her in talent, understanding, warmth and humility was Edith Wynne Matthison.

It was nothing less than shocking and it took Meredith some time to work out exactly what had happened to turn this unremarkable woman into the sort of person one could not take one's eyes off. She had always thought her own presence, her height, her stature, her natural ability to command attention was all an actress needed on stage. It was her unique gift, one she was born with, that she'd never had to work on or nurture. It had simply never occurred to Meredith that acting, the business of pretending to be another person, required anything more than effectively turning up to rehearsals and learning lines. But *this*. This was quite different.

Then there was Barker himself. Again he appeared to do very little. On the face of it he seemed to leave the actors to themselves, intervening only occasionally and usually, as he himself confessed almost apologetically, to tell them not to do a thing. At times he would use a musical analogy, as in 'We need a clarinet here rather than an oboe'. He directed the Trafalgar Square scene like an orchestra – balancing between the speakers and the hecklers as a conductor does between the woodwind and the strings, making sure the right person was heard at the right time. It took a lot of hard work and precision to make the whole thing look spontaneous.

Now and then he prompted the actors to *listen* to their fellow players, to remind them they were hearing the words for the very first time. Again and again he would cut a line he considered unnecessary, always with the charming explanation that the eloquence of the performer conveyed the meaning clearly enough without the need for words. At the same time should anyone misplace a speech, or speak a line or a word that was not in the script, he was onto them like a benign tiger, always emphasising the playwright was king. (Or in this instance, queen.)

Meredith was not used to this kind of scrutiny. The person in charge of getting a play onto the stage, generally known as the producer, was in her experience the actor-manager of the theatre such as Herbert Tree, who was largely concerned with whether or not an actor could be heard. Tree himself was renowned for playing fast and loose with the script, as it suited him, rarely speaking the same words in every performance – in order, was his reasoning, to keep the work fresh. (In truth he found learning lines unnecessarily tiresome.) The idea of *studying* a character, of getting under the skin, of *living* in another person's shoes, of in effect turning a theatrical performance into something resembling real life, was revolutionary in Meredith's experience.

She began to see why actors fought one another for the opportunity to work with Barker. Why otherwise run-of-the-mill performers consistently turned out top-notch performances at the Court and nowhere else. They worked hard enough at it. In the brief three weeks of rehearsal they worked well into the night, every night. They were exhausted, almost dead on their feet. But not one of them complained.

When Edith Wynne Matthison approached Meredith one day in a break in rehearsals to ask, sweetly, why she was present at every rehearsal even when she was not required, Meredith was rendered momentarily and uncharacteristically speechless.

'I like to watch you work,' she was able to stammer. 'You are . . .' Here she hesitated. She wanted to say something like 'revelatory', but praise was not something Meredith handed out easily, if at all, let alone the kind of idolatrous gush that so many in her profession were prone to.

'I like to attend all the rehearsals,' she said, lamely.

Miss Wynne Matthison's eyes twinkled. 'Got your eye on my part?' she said. 'Of course you have, clever girl.' She winked.

'This woman,' she went on. 'What a saint, eh? To tell the truth I didn't want to go near her at the beginning, the sanctimonious so-and-so. The audience would hate her, I thought. But then there was Harley and, well, who turns down the offer to work with Harley?'

She looked at Meredith closely. 'Your first time?'

'My first . . . Oh, you mean at the Court, with . . . Why yes.'

'He's a magician, don't you agree? There's no one else like him, no one in the world. Once you've worked with Harley you don't want to work with anyone else.' Then, as if reading Meredith's thought and with a marginally theatrical sigh, 'Such a shame he is only recently married,' she said. Then she winked again, and with a dramatic swish of her skirt she turned on her heel and resumed her place at the centre of the rehearsal room.

8: Votes for Women

The first performance drew an audience to rival any West End opening, including the playwrights J M Barrie and Arthur Wing Pinero and Emmeline Pankhurst herself and her daughters.

The audience was noisy, at times boisterously so. The close of the second act drew boos from the gallery and shouts of approval and stamping from supporters in the stalls at the same time.

The reviews, written exclusively by men, were mixed. 'Not so much a play as a political tract' was the general consensus. Some described the play as melodramatic, absurd, formless and overlong. Others seemed confused as to whether they were supposed to be reviewing the Cause or the Play; the first of which they on the whole were reluctant to comment on. Many of them took objection to the notion that all men were regarded as evil good-for-nothings, and one reviewer referred to the suffragettes as 'a plaguy nuisance' and 'shrieking women', which alone was enough to make Meredith bristle with indignation but not quite enough to persuade her to espouse the cause.

As 'an exercise on feminine logic warmed by the glow of feminine sympathy and the fire of feminine wrath' it was thought both moving and beautiful. And such was the power of its central performance even the critics were able for a brief spell to ignore the ludicrousness of the plot. The acting overall received fulsome praise, as was expected at the Court, and to a man the reviewers fell head over heels for Edith Wynne Matthison.

But the highlight of the whole event was by unanimous agreement the second act, which according to one reviewer was the most remarkable piece of staging he had ever seen in a theatre. 'Whoever is responsible for it is a genius in the art', declared the man from *The Globe*.

The fact that the subject of abortion was alluded to only obliquely – for fear of offending the censor, who had already banned Granville Barker's play *Waste* for being rather more forthright on the same topic – caused some confusion among many reviewers. As an exercise in propaganda the play was unlikely to advance the cause of female suffrage, was the general view, due not least to the central character of Vida Levering who, despite Miss Wynne Matthison's sympathetic portrayal, showed herself to be both stupid and stone-hearted when she turned down an offer of marriage for the sake of her Belief. A remark that, in Meredith's view, was *almost* enough to turn any mildly intelligent person into a suffragette.

~

For Merry, despite the frustration of having to sit out most of the play backstage, it was a thrill to be involved in the best scene in the play Everyone Was Talking About. She spent most of the first and third acts languishing in her dressing room, which she shared with far too many of her fellow actresses. Just occasionally she would venture into the cramped (and crowded) green room where she would pretend to read the newspaper, or perhaps a book, while her fellow thesps indulged in card games or backgammon and she secretly eavesdropped, or conjured up ways of bringing about the accidental demise of Edith Wynne

Matthison.

Nobody took much notice of her, nor she of them. Banter did not interest Meredith and there was a lot of banter backstage. The only one who tried to draw her into conversation was Bertie, real name Sidney but commonly known as Bertie for some reason, and on occasion Queen Bertie.

Meredith found the idea of homosexuality puzzling yet fascinating. There was, as the saying goes, a lot of it around in the theatre business, as she had quickly discovered. Homosexuals, or queens, or whatever one liked to call them, were on the whole much easier to get along with as they posed no threat to a woman; indeed for the most part they thought like a woman, one could have such a cosy chat with a homosexual without the slightest hint of envy or competitiveness creeping in. At the same time one could not ignore the fact that it was not so long since the most famous homosexual of all, the playwright and wit Oscar Wilde, had been publicly exposed as a 'sodomite' and spent two years in prison for it. So one could express surprise that the likes of Queen Bertie made absolutely no secret of his sexual proclivities, indeed he quite openly flaunted them.

He told Meredith the story of how he had once been hauled up before a magistrate accused of 'a lewd act'. When he politely asked for details the magistrate shifted uncomfortably, brought out his watch, looked at it, replaced it in his pocket and pronounced, 'You know exactly to what we are referring.'

'But milord, forgive me but I believe I need it to be spelled out. You see, I am just a common man and unless you can explain to me precisely what the charges are, why, how can I know whether to plead guilty or not guilty?'

The magistrate hummed and hawed a while longer and

then peered at Bertie beneath his eyebrows and said, 'The location was Hampstead Heath, the complainant was a young man. Need I explain further?'

'Hampstead Heath? Oh, you mean the time I was lost and asked directions of a stranger, I do remember. Is that a lewd act?'

The magistrate continued to regard him steadily for a few moments. 'I believe you did more than ask directions.'

'Did I? I don't recall. Perhaps you can remind me.'

'Mr Symonds, I was not there, so I cannot tell you precisely what occurred, except that it concerned a large tree.'

'My word, where does the tree come into it?'

'You tell me.'

'I would if I could recall the tree. What kind of tree was it?'

The magistrate raised his voice several levels. 'The tree is immaterial. The fact is, according to a witness, it was the location of the lewd act.'

'Well, tell the truth sir, I am flummoxed. If asking directions is regarded as a lewd act, tree or no tree, then I am lost. In every sense.'

Merry didn't believe a word of it. But the idea that a defendant could be let off because he was unable to defend himself against an act the magistrate was unable to spell out amused her mightily. At the same time one should never forget that men like Bertie walked a tightrope every minute of the day. Why even his walk gave him away, let alone his clothes, to say nothing of his mannerisms.

When meant, so Meredith concluded, homosexuals had to be the bravest people on earth.

There was a good deal of toing and froing in the green room on the topic of women's suffrage, of course. When

Meredith expressed doubts about it on the grounds that women had not been sufficiently educated in politics to know what really went on in parliament the company *en masse* descended upon her with cries of 'shame on you' for betraying the sisterhood. Inwardly she acknowledged she was playing devil's advocate to some extent in order to prove she was not following the herd like the rest of them. Outwardly, she remonstrated, she queried the notion that women would advance their cause by joining an outdated men's club.

All that diversion aside, the time went all too quickly. The play was packed out, with audience members standing three rows deep, queues around the block and scores of people turned away at every performance. The eight scheduled matinees were extended and later on the play was moved to the evening. Audience members were a good deal less critical of the play than the reviewers. One or two of them even asked for Meredith's autograph at the stage door (she suspected they did not know who she was but she signed them anyway, with a gracious smile, as befits the leading lady she considered herself to be). The play's run only terminated when the management team of Vedrenne and Barker's contract with the Court came to an end in the summer.

9: Two ladies discuss the play

'Gracious me, you call that a play?' sniffed Mrs Henry Gulliver. 'It was more like a sermon on politics.'

'That is more or less as the writer described it Susanna dear,' said Mrs Maurice Stephenson. 'It called itself a "dramatic tract".'

'Hmm.' Susanna took a sip of her tea. She was seated with her friend at a corner table at Tiffany's teashop in Sloane Street, around the corner from the Court Theatre. She had only agreed to accompany Virginia to the matinée of *Votes for Women* because she happened to be free that day, and because it was just a short stroll from her front door in Eaton Square. Susanna tolerated the West End theatre, not least because it was a way to catch up with friends. But the Court was something entirely different, why the audience was positively drab, and obviously happy to put up with drab plays about drab subjects. At the same time she was curious to witness Virginia's daughter live on stage, which she thought might be interesting but in the event turned out to be a disappointment.

'Remind me,' she said, dabbing at her lips and glancing around at the other customers, 'which one was Meredith?'

'She was part of the crowd in Trafalgar Square. The tall one, in green, standing at the side on the right.'

'Ah,' said Susanna.

'With the carrying voice.'

Susanna's attention had been mostly held through the first act, Virginia surmised, and slightly less so during the second. By act three she was definitely fidgeting.

'To tell you the truth,' said Susanna. 'I found it hard to follow. All those words. Remind me what it was about.'

And so Virginia recapped for the benefit of her inattentive friend the gist of the story, and in particular of the third act. How Geoffrey Stoner, with ambitions to become a Cabinet member, on being confronted unexpectedly by his one-time lover – whose baby she had aborted many years earlier in order to save his career – offers to make amends by marrying her, even though he is engaged to someone else; and how she in return dismisses his offer but insists instead that he commit to the cause of women's suffrage, thereby throwing his political ambitions overboard.

'She did what?'

'She refused his offer. Instead she demanded he sign the telegram in support of female suffrage.'

'She refused him? Silly girl,' Susanna pulled a face. 'And he was so good-looking.'

'That was the point, Susanna dear,' said Virginia. 'That is why it was described as a "tract".'

'I don't remember any mention of . . . you know.'

'What?'

'Well, it was never exactly spoken out loud, was it?'

'What are you talking about?'

'The death of the child, from . . .'

'The abortion.'

'Well!' Susanna mock-fanned her face with her hand. 'I mean, how is one to understand what she is trying to say? All that hating men business. I do think female suffrage is such a waste of time. Why do I need to vote when I can get Henry to vote for me?'

'You mean you tell him who to vote for?'

'Of course.'

'And how do you know he does? How do you know what he does when he gets to the polling station?'

'Virginia dear, you are quite naïve sometimes.'

'Maybe.' Virginia sighed.

A while ago Virginia might have agreed with her friend. What was the point of female suffrage? She found the prospect of voting really quite intimidating. Yet she had found the play oddly moving, and especially the second act. It was not just because her own daughter played a part in it – a very small part, rather to Virginia's surprise – it was the extraordinary effect of seeing a full-scale rally taking place in Trafalgar Square with a crowd numbering twenty or more on the tiny stage of the Court Theatre. You would not have thought it possible to reconstruct something that felt so utterly *real*. In a strange way it was more real than reality itself, so *cleverly* staged, and every character in that scene was a distinct person. She believed in every one of them, even her own daughter.

It also occurred to her, with some shock, that it was the first time she had witnessed common people portrayed, with compassion and seriousness, on stage.

'What are you thinking?' enquired her friend.

'Didn't you find the second act extraordinary?' said Virginia. 'I was utterly transported. You know it made me want to see it for myself, to witness a real-life rally. They were so . . .' she searched for the word, '*passionate*. And not one of them was the sort of person you'd expect them to be. Especially the young one, and the lady playing Vida – oh!' Here Virginia clasped her hands together, 'what an actress! *What* an actress!'

Her friend stared at her. 'Don't get too carried away Ginger,' she said. 'Remember they were only actors. Suffragettes don't really look like that.'

'How do you know? Have you ever seen one?'

'Not precisely, but . . .'

'They look exactly like anyone else. Besides, what does it matter what they look like?'

'Please don't tell me you're becoming sympathetic to the cause, darling.'

'Well, why not? No, of course not. I am just curious, that's all.' She stirred her tea thoughtfully.

'Because honestly dearest, women have far more important things to do. Henry used to joke that men took care of the important things in life, such as earning a living and choosing Prime Ministers, while women looked after the everyday stuff, such as how the children should be brought up and in what sort of surroundings and with whom they should associate. And honestly, darling,' here she leaned over to all but whisper in Virginia's ear, 'I told him I concur absolutely.' She laughed merrily. 'Only I beg the question as to who is more important. Women already have the power, only men don't realise it. Why should we be bothered by the vote? What difference is it going to make to our everyday lives?'

Virginia did not have a ready answer to that one. Would the vote have made it any easier for her to have gone to the stage door and asked to see her daughter? Or, more pertinently, to have confessed to her husband she had watched their daughter performing on stage and stood up to his inevitable fury? Not directly, of course not. And yet this business of one sex being more important, more in control, than another made absolutely no sense at all when you thought about it.

Ultimately, if she had the vote, would it make her

husband treat her any differently? Of course not. Or would it?

'I must say,' her friend continued, 'and forgive me, but I was surprised to see your Meredith playing such a small part.'

Although the more she thought about it the more sense it made. It would certainly add to one's own feelings of self-importance, and maybe even encourage men, husbands in particular, to treat their wives a little less patronisingly. She knew of several women who were infinitely more intelligent and thoughtful than their husbands.

'Ginger?'

'I'm sorry, I was miles away. What did you say?'

'I was just saying I found it surprising that Meredith should have given up so much to play such a small part.'

And would the vote have any effect on the relationships between women? Would it make one feel less defensive?

She did not want to dignify her friend's remark with a response. So she smiled at her and sipped her tea, and resolved to find out where and when the next rally was due to take place in support of female suffrage.

10: The biggest gathering in the world

'You're going where?' demanded Virginia's husband.

'To Hyde Park,' said Virginia. 'I am attending a rally in support of the suffragettes.'

She had rehearsed this scene so many times she almost felt it had actually happened. She had anticipated the response, she was ready with her answers.

'Are you out of your mind? They are a liability, to themselves, and to everyone around them. What in God's name gave you this idea? Or rather who? Was it Tony the Honker? I bet it was the Honker. How typical. Well I forbid it.'

'You can't forbid it Maurice, I am your wife not your daughter.'

'For your own safety, woman!'

'I know how to take care of myself, dearest. Please do not concern yourself. You are welcome to come too, if you think I need your protection.' She smiled at him. As rehearsed scenes went, it was proceeding predictably. She felt reassuringly calm.

'Well, I'm blowed if I . . . In any case I've made previous arrangements, as you already know.'

'That's a shame.' She did her best to look crestfallen.

'Well.' He blustered to himself, and stroked his moustache, and looked at her curiously, as if he wasn't quite sure who she was. 'Well at least take Carrington with you. He will drive you there and I'll make sure he stays close by your side throughout.'

He turned to gaze around him as if he didn't quite recognise where he was, even though he was standing right by his fireside in his very own living room. Virginia felt almost sorry for him.

'Very well dear,' she said.

On the whole it had been easier than she anticipated, and she'd only had to commandeer one direct lie and one evasion, that she agreed to the chauffeur staying by her side throughout the whole event and that her friend Antonia – nicknamed Tony the Honker so cruelly by her husband due to what he viewed as her forthright manner and her bizarre laugh – would indeed be accompanying her.

~

A bird looking down on London at midday on 21 June 1908 would have spotted a number of pools of what looked like white flowers on the banks of the Thames and to the north, west and centre of the city. After a while the pools began to dissolve into streams, snaking slowly through the streets of London in the same direction, as if the Thames had flooded and created tributaries. Just north of central London those tributaries, swollen now to twice their size, flowed through a number of gates to eventually form one vast lake inside Hyde Park.

Swooping down to ground level the bird would have identified the flowers as women dressed almost entirely in white, with sashes and scarves in purple and green. Some of them carried banners with slogans such as 'Keep on pestering!' or '54 weeks in Holloway Gaol'. At the head of the processions were marching bands and policemen on horseback. Looking more closely our curious bird would have made out a motley gathering of old and young, male as well as female, some carrying infants or pushing perambulators, others in wheelchairs; some smartly dressed, others not, and marching alongside them groups of policemen keeping a close eye on the gaggles of young men they suspected might be Up To No Good.

~

It had taken a good hour for the crowd in Trafalgar Square to even get moving, by which time Meredith was already thinking about giving up and going home. She was there, needless to say, under sufferance, because in the end it had been easier to agree to go than to yet again have to explain herself to her fellow actors as the only member of the cast of *Votes for Women* who was not intending to attend the rally.

Instructions had been for the women to wear white, with purple and green accessories. So as a statement of independence with just a modicum of solidarity with the cause Merry wore a white blouse with a dark blue skirt and a magnificent hat trimmed especially for the occasion in shades of blue and red. Bertie, in breeches, white tights and purple waistcoat 'purloined from wardrobe, darling', was by her side, which made the whole thing a little more tolerable.

'*Courage, ma petite*,' he said.

When they finally got to move off along Pall Mall they went as a group, the entire cast of *Votes for Women*, headed by Elizabeth Robins carrying a banner declaring, appropriately enough, 'Votes for women!' She was accompanied by Edith Wynne Matthison and Lillah McCarthy, husband Granville Barker alongside. Some of the bystanders, recognising the two actresses, let out a cheer. As they marched – for it was a march, it was made clear these women were going to war – so the pace slowed as many of the bystanders joined them. Bertie kept a firm hold on Meredith's arm, 'To prevent you from bolting, dear,' he said.

~

It became obvious within moments of leaving St Leonard's Terrace that there was no way a vehicle could find its way through the traffic to Hyde Park. King's Road was already blocked off and no amount of remonstration between Carrington and the policeman on duty could persuade him to allow them to cross it.

'There's nothing for it ma'am but I'm going to have to take a detour west, or maybe east of Sloane Square,' said the chauffeur, as he swung the wheel around.

'Carrington, stop here a minute,' said Virginia.

They were in the middle of the road around the corner from St Leonard's Terrace. Carrington drew up by the kerb.

'Leave me here,' said Virginia.

The chauffeur turned in his seat. 'I beg your pardon madam, but I have strict instructions . . .'

'I know you do. But I have even stricter ones. Leave me here. I will find my own way there and back again. This is about as close as you could get to the park anyway.'

'Madam, I cannot do that.' He was almost leaping out of his seat now. 'Brigadier Stephenson insisted . . .'

'Never mind the brigadier. Take the afternoon off. Drive around London – do what you like for a few hours, but don't go home. I will cover for you.'

'I cannot let you do this.'

'Carrington,' she placed a hand on his arm. 'I will be perfectly all right. I am a sensible woman, you know that, I can take care of myself.'

And with that she opened the car door and let herself out before the poor man could stop her.

It was as well she had made a prior arrangement to meet her friend Antonia in Markham Street. Left to her own devices she would have suggested a spot in Hyde Park, but Tony was an old hand at this.

'We'd never find one another Ginnie, believe me.'

If it can be said that opposites attract, nowhere did that apply more than with Virginia and her friends. Being a woman of wobbly conviction she attracted around her people who were shall we say prone to bossiness. As meek people often bring out the assertiveness in their closest companions, so Virginia's vagueness somehow drew to her people, women in particular, who were quite the opposite.

Susanna was a case in point: a woman who would never allow something as inconvenient as her husband's objections stop her doing exactly what she wanted to do. Likewise, though in a very different way, Antonia was a woman of clear-sighted practicality, certainly when it came to attending rallies.

She was waiting for her as planned on the corner of Markham Street and King's Road. She was dressed from head to toe in white: white dress, white gloves, white hat with purple sash and, incongruously, wielding a pink parasol. As she spotted Virginia hesitating on the opposite side of the blocked-off King's Road she waved her parasol and shouted, 'Bravo!', before barging through the phalanx of police to rescue her and drag her back across the street. From there she marched her friend up Markham Street, still clutching her elbow, just as the first lines of mounted police approached along the King's Road at the head of one of the many processions of white, green and purple.

They continued up Markham Street away from the procession, zigzagging through side roads at a pace, while Antonia kept up a running commentary of how they could avoid the masses and make their own way to Hyde Park, she had thought it all through and planned it accordingly, and trust me dear Ginnie I do know what I'm doing.

'I'm sure you do,' panted Virginia.

'Am I going too fast for you? There, slow down, catch your breath, there's really no need to rush. You know they are expecting upwards of one hundred thousand, that is a lot of people Ginnie, I hope you're up to it.'

'I hope so too,' said her friend.

'How was it with Maurice? I imagine he objected, of course he did, how did you manage to give him the slip? Do you know he once tried to recruit me into his battalion?' She honked with laughter. 'He said I'd make an ideal sergeant major, can you imagine? What a card, eh?'

Much of Antonia's monologue was, needless to say, rhetorical.

'Did he mention me? I suppose he did. I know he doesn't approve of me, though in an odd way he quite admires me too. I believe he thinks of me as a chum, a male chum that is, but I don't quite fit.' She honked again.

No matter what one thought of Antonia she was an amusing companion, and the fact she never seemed to expect or request a response to her constant prattle made it easier for Virginia simply to follow her leader on the journey through Cadogan Square and Hans Place towards Knightsbridge.

'Ever been to a rally before? No, I don't suppose you have. Excellent weather for it, there may well turn out to be more than one hundred thousand, and then who can ignore us! We're all but home and dry Ginnie, if they pretend not to hear us this time we can no longer call ourselves a democracy.'

They reached the park while there were only a few people milling about, as Antonia had planned and predicted, and at her insistence they took up position near one of the many platforms erected for the various speakers. 'With a bit of luck, if I've planned it right, this will be Christabel's', Antonia announced. 'She's an excellent speaker, spirited, more so than her mama, in my opinion.' Then, with barely a pause, she turned to a small group of young lads who were lurking nearby and asked, 'Are you supporters of the cause? Of course you are, otherwise why would you be here? How excellent. We need the young blood, especially the male variety.'

As she turned away she did not see, though her companion did, those same young lads bursting into laughter and making what Virginia could only assume, being a protected species herself, extremely rude gestures.

~

By the time Meredith and her group arrived the park was already heaving. In the distance she spotted above the heads of the crowds what appeared to be platforms or wagons with people upon them addressing the crowds, or so she imagined because nobody who was not within shouting distance of those platforms could possibly hear what was being said. There was a general atmosphere of jollity in the air; children played, people picnicked, it was as if a good deal of the attendees were there simply for the sake of a day out on a glorious June afternoon.

After several minutes of 'hanging about' she clutched hold of Bertie's sleeve and said, 'What are we doing, standing here doing nothing? I want to hear what they're saying.' With which she pulled him after her and forced her way through the throngs until they were just about within earshot of the woman on the platform, whom Bertie informed her was no less than Christabel Pankhurst herself.

'Who?'

'Dear child,' sighed Bertie. 'You lead far too sheltered a life.'

~

There had been several other speakers before Christabel Pankhurst made her appearance, at which point Antonia dug an elbow into Virginia's ribs and said, 'See? Right first time, as I said.' Emmeline Pankhurst's eldest daughter began by telling the crowd the story of how she and her fellow suffragette Annie Kenney had once been thrown out of a Liberal Party election campaign meeting in Manchester for asking Sir Edward Grey, the principal speaker, whether his party if elected would adopt female suffrage; and how when they told the crowd outside the meeting room what had happened they were promptly arrested 'for assaulting police officers' and gaoled for a week. 'That, ladies and gentleman,' said Christabel, 'is what we are up against. So far as politics, or women's rights, or opinion of any kind are concerned women are invisible. And we will remain so until we get the vote.'

'Such a slip of a thing,' murmured Virginia. And she was. She could not have been less like the general stereotype of the suffragette, with her fine features and her voice: clear, refined, precise, and here and there emphatic. 'Dear Maurice, if only you could see her,' muttered Virginia.

'What's that?' demanded Antonia. 'Did you mention Maurice? I told Desmond you might not be allowed to escape, he said the trouble with Maurice is he's stuck in the 18th century, and he's right. Des wanted to come along and I told him, that's all very well but you're not coming with me. He may well be here now, for all I know.' She looked around as if expecting to spot her husband amid the hordes of people. 'How many of us are there, I wonder?' she asked of no one in particular. 'The whole world seems to have turned out, absolutely splendid. They cannot ignore us now, they simply cannot.'

'. . . We who have comfortable homes may ask what difference will the vote make to my perfectly pleasant existence?' Miss Pankhurst continued. 'The answer depends on those around you. Does your family respect your opinion on current events, for example? Does your family even know what your opinions are? But far more importantly, what about those of us who do not have comfortable homes? Who may not have a home at all? It could be any one of us, by a break in fortune. Many women in the workhouses today are widows who were left destitute on the death of their husbands, often with children to support. Decent, law-abiding women, middle-class and working-class, condemned to spend the rest of their lives scrubbing floors and living on subsistence, simply because they have no voice.'

'Oh my dear,' exclaimed Virginia.

'What about the young girl, a scullery maid, who was thrown out of the house by her employer, the baby's father, and then convicted of murder when the baby died, while the father went scot free? What about the young girls, thirteen and fourteen year-olds, who are seeking assistance for their illegitimate babies, often fathered by their own father or another close relative? Who is going to help these women if they have no voice? If you ask, as many people do, why we are willing to go to prison for our beliefs, that is why.'

This produced prolonged cheers from the crowd, except for a group of young lads – the same group Antonia had addressed when they first arrived – who hooped and hollered and yelled 'Nobody asked you to do it, you stupid woman,' and 'Get back home to your husband, if you have one, he'll tell you what's what.' At which, to the alarm and amusement of the crowd Antonia, deploying her parasol as a weapon, laid about those young lads with such ferocity they cowered and yelped and pleaded for mercy as she swiped and poked and slapped them about the head, and may have continued to do so for some time had a couple of policemen not stepped in and grabbed hold of the troublemakers, 'for your own protection, lads,' and removed them. When one of the policemen then attempted to wrest Antonia's parasol from her grip she started to lay about him, until her friend Virginia stepped in and, with uncharacteristic firmness, snatched the parasol from her friend's hand and, with a gracious smile and an abject apology to the official 'on my friend's behalf', managed to calm her down.

All of which provided a temporary diversion from the speakers and won Antonia and Virginia a spontaneous round of applause.

It was at this point that Meredith, peering over the heads of the crowd to see what was going on the far side of the podium, got the shock of her life.

'What's up dearest, did you see a ghost?' Bertie enquired.

'Yes,' said Merry. 'I just saw my mother.'

11: Mrs Vlatsky's conundrum

Mrs Vlatsky was not a happy woman. She did not like having to write letters to Meredith's mother about what her daughter was up to without her daughter knowing, she felt like a spy and a sneak. She was not a naturally deceitful person and while she did not feel the need to lie directly to her lodger – and surrogate daughter, as Mrs Stephenson herself had described her – having to keep secrets from her was in Mrs Vlatsky's mind much the same thing.

So when it came to passing on news she was selective. She informed Mrs Stephenson about Meredith's health, both physical and to some extent mental, as in 'she has ups and downs, like us all', and of course about her professional engagements, which is how Meredith's mother came to know about her role at the Court Theatre. About Merry's personal life, which is to say her romantic life, she was cagey, and occasionally fanciful, as in 'she has many admirers but they do not seem to interest her,' which was truer in Mrs V's imagination than in real life. She regarded Merry as an attractive young woman who by definition would have plenty of male admirers. The fact that they did not come to call meant, in Mrs Vlatsky's mind, that she did not encourage them to do so.

Meredith's love life was bewildering, in Mrs V's eyes.

Could a young woman these days turn her back on love and marriage for the sake of a career? It did not make a lot of sense. Yet it did seem odd that in all the conversations they had had Merry had never mentioned a male admirer, and when questioned on the topic she had simply shrugged and said something to the effect that the only men who interested her were unavailable (married, in other words), and that most of the men she fraternised with were actors and as anyone with brain was aware, actors made useless husbands.

Then there was the money. It arrived regularly on the first of every month. It was enough to cover Meredith's rent and a little over. And what was Mrs V to do with that? She could not give it to Merry directly. She had tried, once, and been firmly rebuffed. 'Thank you Mrs Vlatsky, it's most kind of you but I will not be in receipt of handouts.' So she had to find other ways of indulging her lodger, such as walnut cake, home-baked, or pigeon pie or other delicacies, especially bought from Harrods or Selfridge's, since pastry was not one of Mrs V's fortes. Once she produced a fine silk scarf which she swore she'd been given by a distant cousin, with 'No, it is not for me, the colour is not good for me,' and trinkets, pieces of semi-precious jewellery which Meredith graciously accepted and never wore. It was quite a trial one way or another.

Then there was the time when Meredith fell into such a deep gloom that Mrs Vlatsky became positively worried. It began after she'd attended the suffragette rally in Hyde Park. She had arrived home at the end of the day exhausted and without a word to her landlady had taken to her room and refused to leave it for an entire day.

Should she inform Meredith's mother? Mrs V agonised. She read the cards, but they were no help. When Merry did eventually emerge, driven by hunger, she cooked her a hearty breakfast and enquired anxiously after her health.

Merry looked at Mrs V with hooded eyes. 'Since when did you take it upon yourself to feed me, Mrs Vlatsky?' she asked sleepily. 'You are an angel in strange clothing,' she added, a touch obscurely.

'I am concerned for you, my dear,' said the good lady. 'You are not well. We should have the doctor.'

'No need, Mrs V,' said Meredith. 'Thank you. Just a touch of exhaustion, nothing more.'

~

It was not exhaustion so much as shock. It felt as if all Meredith's faculties had suddenly decided to shut down. That the sight of her mother at the suffragette rally should have such an effect came as a total surprise, and all the more unwelcome to a person who likes to think she is control of things. It was truly like seeing a ghost.

She had felt faintly sick, and weirdly weak. Bertie, God bless him, had helped her out of the crowd to a bench in a quiet spot under a beech tree, where he sat her down and, without asking questions, stayed with her until some of her strength had returned. He had then walked with her to Knightsbridge where he hailed a cab and rode with her to her front door where, again without questions, he left her. She had then, as aforesaid, gone straight to her bedroom where she lay down on the bed and remained there throughout the evening and most of the following night staring at the ceiling, before she fell into a deep sleep that lasted fourteen hours.

~

Meredith's mother planned her conversation on the way home from the rally. (She was prone to planning conversations was Virginia, especially in tricky situations.)

True to her forethoughtfulness Antonia, bless her, had organised for the two of them to be picked up in a pre-organised cab just behind Harrods. On their way back to St Leonard's Terrace and while Antonia prattled merrily on about this and that, Virginia contemplated the best way to placate what she anticipated to be an irritated and irate husband.

'Would you like me to come in with you?' asked Antonia as the cab drew up outside the house.

'I don't think so Antonia if you don't mind. I'm not sure if I have seen you yet today.' Her friend gave her an odd look as Virginia stepped down from the carriage. 'But thank you once again, for everything. It was most enlightening.'

'And amusing,' said Antonia. 'Will you tell Maurice about the little fracas with the policemen?'

'That would be difficult if you weren't there,' said Virginia.

Antonia nodded. 'A shame. I thought it might raise me slightly in his books.'

Virginia smiled and gave her friend's hand a squeeze before she turned towards her house.

The problem with lies, she pondered as she hesitated on the doorstep, is that they are so much more complicated than the truth. Lies have to be consistent where the truth, paradoxically, doesn't. And while in the relatively short time it had taken them to get from Knightsbridge to St Leonard's Terrace she had conjured up three different scenarios: Carrington had stayed by her side throughout, as promised, and everything went according to plan; she had dismissed Carrington because of difficulties with traffic and had proceeded on her own, and from then everything had gone according to plan; she had dismissed Carrington because he could not get through the traffic and had met up with a group of friends and everything had gone according to plan. What she hadn't contemplated was the truth. And the truth was in the circumstances so much more straightforward and so much more amusing. And after all, the only reason she had denied meeting up with Antonia in the first place was out of pique: because of her husband's exasperating habit of referring to her as Tony the Honker, which was downright insulting, even if true, and drove her to distraction; and were she to refer to any of his friends in such a manner he would be frankly apoplectic.

'Hello darling,' she said gaily as she entered the drawing room.

12: As others see us

They had arranged to meet at the very bench in Hyde Park upon which Bertie had deposited Meredith after she all but passed out at the suffragette rally. 'To lay the ghost,' he said, with intentional irony.

'I thought you were being mildly melodramatic, my dear. Most people don't faint at the sight of their mothers. Although I would, since she's been gone these past twelve years.'

Meredith gazed wanly into the middle distance. It was July, still warm if not quite as sunny as the day of the rally – Women's Sunday it came to be called. She was watching two small children playing hide and seek, zigzagging through the trees, shrieking with laughter.

'I haven't seen her for four years,' she said.

A dog tried to join in the game, leaping from tree to tree, now chasing the boy, now the girl, while its owner looked on, shouting occasionally and pointlessly.

'They threw me out of the house when I said I wanted to be a professional actress,' said Meredith. 'I didn't think they meant it at the time.'

Bertie nodded.

'And I don't think they thought I meant it either. But there we are. My father's a brigadier,' she added, as if that explained things, which it partly did of course. 'And now look at me.'

Bertie turned to do so. 'And what am I seeing?'

'Well,' she shrugged. 'I gave up my family and my home, and here I am. I thought by now I'd be, you know.'

'You'd be what?'

'I would be something. Something on the West End stage. If not a leading lady. But at least working all the time, playing wonderful parts.'

'Of haughty ladies,' said Bertie.

'That's unfair.' Meredith felt oddly near to tears, which was torturous.

'But then you play the haughty lady so well, my dear,' said Bertie.

The dog's owner had given up and was now in friendly conversation with the children's minder, sharing a joke perhaps about the intricacies of coping with children and dogs.

'You didn't enter the profession because you thought it was fair, did you? Whoever told you that? Dear me,' Bertie sighed. 'Young people,' he added, and shook his head.

'What do you mean?'

'My father disowned me too,' he said. 'Not because I wanted to tread the boards, but for other reasons.' He looked up to study the branches of the tree above him. Meredith waited.

'The problem with young people,' he continued eventually, 'you think all it takes is passion. And sacrifice. "If I do this, if I suffer that, then things will fall into place."' He chuckled. 'If success were the natural result of sacrifice and suffering – my word, what a lot of S's! – every penniless orphan in the world would be a leading actor, or a top scientist. Or who knows what.'

Meredith frowned. Then, 'Why did your father disown you, Bertie?' she asked.

'Why do you think?'

There was a brief hiatus as Meredith pondered on Bertie's remark.

'Is that how you see me, Bertie? As a haughty lady?'

'Oh my dear girl.' He took hold of her hand and laid it proprietorially on his lap.

'You know, people used to call me Merry. That's how I was always known.'

Bertie nodded again. He stroked her hand.

'I changed it to Meredith because I thought people would take me more seriously.'

'Well,' said Bertie.

She felt suddenly ashamed. Here was she, Miss Privilege, who'd chosen a career over her family and paid a price for it. Bertie on the other hand – what sort of price did he have to pay, day after day, for simply being who he was?

'How do you get through the day, Bertie?' she asked, after a long moment.

'Good gracious,' he shrugged dramatically. 'What sort of a question is that? How does anyone? You put the trials and tribulations into a back room, where you can't see them, close the door and forget all about them and get on with the day.'

How he could remain so positive was remarkable. She felt mildly jealous.

'So your mother is a suffragette, is she? That's very modern,' he said.

'It's very surprising. I don't suppose father would approve for a moment. If he knows.' Meredith considered this for a moment. What else had been going on at home these past few years?

'More than her daughter, so it seems,' said Bertie. 'Mind you I wouldn't want to be on the wrong side of those ladies, not for a moment. Fearsome, some of them.'

'Is that so?'

'They have to be. And the more they protest, the louder their voices, the more we simple men tremble in our socks. And that includes our noble Prime Minister I do believe.'

'You think he's afraid of them?'

'Of course. Who wouldn't be?'

Meredith laughed. 'That's a sort of ridiculous suggestion, Bertie.'

'You see that is where you are entirely wrong.'

He turned this time to face her directly. He still had her hand in his, and now he squeezed it and said, 'The world is afraid of Meredith Martin, that's for sure.'

She laughed again, louder this time.

'Which is a shame, because the quieter Meredith Martin, the gentler Meredith Martin, the one I am talking to now, self-pitying though she is, is a different person altogether to the Meredith Martin the world sees.'

'You think so?' She regarded him suspiciously.

'We are actors,' he said. 'We perform on stage, and many of us perform offstage as well, it's in our nature. I do it all the time, as you know. And in time it becomes second nature.' He chortled. 'That's what actors are, of course. Escapees. From themselves, as often as not.'

'You're talking about yourself, are you?'

'Always. Actors always talk about themselves. And if,' he continued before she could interrupt, 'you were to join in the world a little more, step down from your horse, your plinth, wherever it is you have decided to place yourself, join in with the rest of us a little more – you're not so different from everyone else after all, even if you think you are.' With which he replaced her hand in her own lap, as if done with it.

'That's unkind, Bertie,' she said.

'No. You misunderstand me. Dear Meredith, Merry.' He took her face in his hands and kissed her forehead. 'This is exactly what I mean. You think that being no different from other people is a bad thing. It's really awful vanity. Or anxiety, which is often much the same thing. We are all, totally and utterly, different, in much the same way. You see?'

'I'm not sure I do.'

Then, with an impeccable and all but impenetrable Glaswegian accent, he recited:

'"O wad some Power the giftie gie us
To see oursels as ithers see us!
It wad frae mony a blunder free us,
An' foolish notion:
What airs in dress an' gait wad lea'e us,
An' ev'n devotion!"'

'Robbie Burns,' said Meredith. 'I know it.'

'Of course you do, an educated young woman like yourself. And as an educated person you would know only too well how close we all are to ridicule.'

'Who are you talking about now?' she asked.

'All of us,' said Bertie. And then, almost under his breath, he began to mutter the beginning of the poem, rolling the words around his mouth as though they were delicacies.

'"Ha! whaur ye gaun, ye crowlin ferlie?
Your impudence protects you sairly;
I canna say but ye strunt rarely,
Owre gauze and lace;
Tho', faith! I fear ye dine but sparely
On sic a place."

'You see, even smart ladies cannot be wholly protected from the peregrinations of a simple louse,' said Bertie.

~

Haughty, eh?

She stayed put for a while after Bertie left. The children had gone now, as had the dog and its owner. A smart young couple trotted by on horseback along Rotten Row, disturbing the pigeons playing in the sand.

There was a difference between haughtiness and stylishness, was there not? Just because a person walks upright and bears herself well, as her father would say, does not make her haughty. Just because a woman is tall and of necessity is bound to look down on those smaller than her does not mean she looks down on people in general. Does it?

She felt suddenly unnerved. What if everything one had done, or said, in one's life had been misinterpreted? Was pride such a bad thing? Could it be mistaken for conceit? Heavens above, how difficult it was to get things right. Meredith heaved a deep sigh. Oh Bertie, Bertie, what were you trying to tell me?

She thought about her mother. The shock of seeing her in the first place had played havoc with the synapses in her brain. This, her mother's apparent support of women's suffrage, raised all sorts of questions, not least – What would her father have made of it? Or indeed, was her father even aware of it?

To Meredith's knowledge her mother never lied to her husband, although she was quite capable of not telling him everything. Like the little treats she bought for her daughter when they were attending a play, or the silk ribbons she purchased for her from La Rouselle in Jermyn Street. 'Just between you and me,' she would whisper, with a sly giggle. It was a game, and quite harmless, or so her mother assured her. But for her mother to have attended a rally, on her own – although Merry was aware of the woman with her, a boisterous sort, just the kind of woman her mother seemed to attract – without telling her husband was, thought Meredith, unlikely.

What had been going on at St Leonard's Terrace in these past three years? Were her mother and father still together? Was her father still alive? Would anyone have told her if he weren't?

13: Motherhood and daughter

She had told Maurice everything. It was the obvious, and the easiest, thing to do. Yes, she had dismissed Carrington because there was no way a vehicle could make it through the barriers of police around King's Road; and yes she had met up with Antonia (and kindly don't refer to her as Tony the Honker Maurice, you know how much that annoys me). She even told him about Antonia's run-in with the police for laying into a group of unruly mobsters with a parasol, at which Maurice nodded glumly and said, 'I suppose it was her idea all along.'

'What was?'

'The rally business. No doubt it was she who press-ganged you into going in the first place.'

'As a matter of fact, no, it wasn't.'

'Then what put such an idea into your head? Or should I say who?'

He was staring directly at her. She met his gaze, quite calmly. 'Oddly enough Maurice, there are times when I can think for myself,' she said.

So far her husband seemed to be taking things relatively well, almost with resignation. The fact of his wife attending the rally against his wishes had been the initial shock; anything beyond that he appeared to take in his stride. And she was clearly unscathed. As for her motives, that did not truly concern someone like Brigadier Maurice Stephenson, a man of limited imagination, as did not the possibility that his wife of thirty years might for the first time be asserting a kind of independence.

However a small but insistent voice inside Virginia's brain was telling her so far and no further. If her husband ever got wind of the real reason why she first began to take an interest in women's suffrage, which was a play featuring their very own daughter that she had expressly visited the theatre to see, and at the Court Theatre of all places – considered far too radical for the likes of Brigadier Stephenson – not to mention her pilgrimage to Meredith's lodgings and her secret arrangement with their daughter's landlady, then all hell would truly break loose.

If one pondered on the fragility of the life of a woman in Edwardian England, who would not want to campaign for female suffrage? Virginia had led a very comfortable life thus far, thanks to her husband. There had never before been any proper cause for discontent, not about anything important.

Except for the expulsion of their daughter. Their only daughter.

Of course it had hurt at the time, and she had protested, rather feebly now she came to think about it. And got on with things, as one did. That might seem extraordinary to her now, and she did wonder whether had that expulsion taken place today would today's Virginia have gone along with it quite so uncomplainingly as she had done three years ago? And what if she had not? Would her husband have thrown her out of the house as well? And then what?

It gave her a headache just thinking about it. Perhaps the Maurices of this world were right. Women were not made to make important decisions about the running of the country, or even the household. Far better to leave it up to level-headed, clear-sighted men of the world such as Brigadier Stephenson.

Perhaps everything had turned out for the best.

~

Bertie had been right about one thing, Meredith conceded. When one gave up a comfortable home and a loving family, relatively speaking, for one's passion, not out of indulgence but from necessity as one viewed it, there was a certain assumption that one's sacrifice would be rewarded. One denies oneself this, therefore one has a right to that.

She'd never thought of it in this way before, admittedly. The world did not necessarily owe her success in her chosen field. It did not owe her a living. The world owes nothing to someone who frankly has not done a great deal for the world.

Amidst the struggle of family estrangement, and then fighting her way through the labyrinth of dubious theatrical agents and unscrupulous tour managers to finally achieve her ambition of appearing on the West End stage, only to find herself months later apparently back to square one and facing destitution, Meredith had given little thought to the question of whether or not she was actually any good at acting.

She had always believed, or been led to believe, her imposing presence and powerful voice were enough. It was what set her apart from her fellow actresses of what she considered medium stature and modest talent.

So what was it she was not doing right? She was not stupid enough to think the theatre profession was either predictable or fair. She had witnessed enough mediocre performances, even in the West End, to know as much. As for being a team player, which she freely admitted she was not, what did that matter?

But the actual business of acting, of playing a role, of in effect disappearing into someone else, someone possibly not like yourself at all, and being able to convey that person convincingly to an audience of hundreds or even thousands had never preoccupied her to any extent. Not until she had watched Edith Wynne Matthison doing exactly that under the eagle eye of Granville Barker had she begun to grasp what acting really involved. It had been eye-opening and sobering to watch someone who was so far above her in sensibility, talent, understanding and experience. It was the first time Meredith had truly realised there might be more to the business than being the owner of an imposing presence and a powerful voice.

Someone – she forgot who – had once told her 'If you leave the theatre after a performance and can walk past the eager stage-door johnnies unrecognised, *that* is true acting.'

She didn't get it then. What was so admirable about not being recognised? Wasn't that half the point of the whole exercise? Or had she missed the point yet again?

What if she was, fundamentally, untalented? Her 'training', in the form of six months at an elocution academy under the dubious instruction of Willard Featherbridge, a one-time thespian who had trod the boards with Irving and Tree and according to whom acting consisted of the four elements of Stance, Gesture, Voice and Expression, had been hardly auspicious. It was extremely prescriptive, and she had spent much of the following years unlearning it all. Except when it came to Voice, at which she excelled thanks largely to her teacher's emphasis on 'reaching every corner, every crevice of every corner of the largest auditorium without effort', as everyone knows the last thing an audience wants to see is an actor who is trying too hard.

However as Bertie had said through the words of Robbie Burns, we are none of us immune to ridicule. The smartly-dressed gentlewoman piously attending church may well be unknowingly harbouring a louse amid the gauze and lace of her fancy bonnet (and Meredith knew all about fancy bonnets).

What if Meredith's panoply of fancy bonnets had been home to a colony of lice, and she was the only one who was unaware? What if the world had been laughing at her all along?

14: The Stanislavsky masterclass

'Mairie, Mairie, come quickly!' Mrs Vlatsky sounded almost hysterical.

'What is it Mrs V?' Merry called out irritably.

She had been on her way out when she heard the cry from the front room. It was the cards, of course, what else could it be that had thrown Mrs Vlatsky into such a state of high excitement? They had now got to the stage where Meredith's landlady no longer required her presence in order to read the wretched things, she would go through the whole process every morning, regardless.

Meredith peered round the edge of the door to the front room. 'Well?' she said.

It had been a long time since the cards had turned up anything of interest, which is why Meredith no longer felt obliged to sit quietly and watch as her landlady went through the laborious process of laying them out and humming and hawing before as often as not packing them up again with a shake of the head and a 'Nothing today, I am sorry Mairie.'

But today was obviously quite different. Mrs V's smile said everything.

'Look.' She gestured at the cards.

Meredith edged closer to the table. 'What am I looking at?'

'Just look. Here.' Mrs V pointed to a card.

'The Queen of Hearts.'

'Yes!'

'Don't tell me, I am about to meet the man of my dreams.'

'Absolutely so! At last! After all these long long days. It is the first time, the first time since you came to this house. The Queen of Hearts, in so absolutely the right position, it is unmistakable!'

'Well, thank you for that, Mrs Vlatsky.' She turned to go.

'You are not excited?' cried the good woman.

'As a matter of fact . . .' Meredith sighed, and took a breath. 'You know perfectly well Mrs Vlatsky it does not interest me.'

'Oh my dear!'

'I am truly sorry, there is no room in my life for that kind of thing. I am too busy.'

'You are never too busy! A girl cannot be too busy for love!'

'Well this one is. I am sorry Mrs V, I have to go.'

And she did.

~

She was an early arrival at the Criterion Theatre in Piccadilly Circus and she took her seat in the third row of the stalls and fixed her gaze straight ahead of her. So she was unaware of the familiar figure that sat down next to her until it spoke and said, 'Well, if it isn't Magdalena – what was it? – Makepiece. With an "I". Somewhere.'

She turned towards the speaker. For a moment she could not think who he was, let alone what he was talking about.

'Freddy Prentice,' he reminded her. 'That's Freddy with a "y".'

'Ah,' said Meredith.

'On stage at the Court Theatre. Don't tell me you've forgotten it all already.'

Meredith smiled weakly. 'Of course. How are you Freddy Prentice?'

'Hale and hearty,' he said. 'How interesting to see you here. I wouldn't have thought this would be your sort of thing.'

'What do you mean?'

'A lecture on acting.'

'Is that what you call it? Well . . .' she shrugged. 'I had little else on today.'

This was not strictly true. The reason she was really there was because of the metaphorical lice in her hat. Ever since that terrifying conversation with Bertie the very thought of them – or what they represented – had kept her awake at night, so when she heard of the masterclass on a new acting technique said to be taking Russia by storm she felt she owed it to herself to at least go along.

None of this needless to say she was prepared to admit to anyone, Freddy included.

'Well.' Freddy settled himself into his seat and crossed his legs, with some difficulty as Freddy's legs were on the long side and the seats were not sympathetic. 'How have you been?'

Oh God, more small talk. "How have you been? What have you been up to?" Why was it that when one was idle and frankly doing very little that everyone demanded to know your business?

'I've been very well, Freddy, thank you for asking,' she replied coolly before she turned to look straight ahead again.

She'd always found Freddy's cheery friendliness mildly irritating. She would have liked to tell him to mind his own business if such a thing could be done without giving offence.

'I heard about the man from Barker himself,' Freddy informed her. 'I think we are lucky to find ourselves with seats.' He squirmed awkwardly, thanks to his crossed legs, to peer behind at the quickly-filling auditorium. 'He expected to be here himself, so he said.'

'Who did?'

'Barker. Remember him?'

'Of course,' said Meredith.

'No sign of him yet,' Freddy turned back. 'Oomph.' He uncrossed his legs with some effort. 'How much do smart people pay to spend hours in these tiny seats? It's an outrage.'

She was aware of Freddy turning to wave and gesticulate to somebody across the auditorium, yet since she kept her eyes firmly on the stage she was possibly the only person who noticed the man who came bounding on stage like a leopard. A lanky figure dressed from head to foot in black: black hair, unbrushed, the only parts of him that weren't black were his face and his hands, which were clasped before him. He was speaking as he entered, quietly, making no attempt to raise his voice above the hubbub, and he kept on talking as the hubbub lessened and then ceased altogether.

(It was a remarkable entrance: usually a performer waits for the audience to quieten down before starting to speak, at the risk of having to stand still on stage looking faintly foolish. But this method was, thought Meredith, rather remarkable. She might even try it herself some time.)

'Nicholai Androkovsky, assistant to Master Stanislavsky, of Moscow Art Theatre. KS. I am please to be here to talk about Master, welcome.' This with a spread of hands before he clasped them together again. 'Perhaps greatest theatre director in the world, no, I do not exaggerate. Let me tell you about him. Greatest director in the world.'

He paused, and cleared his throat. He spoke reasonably good English, but very very fast and so quietly one had to concentrate on every word. He also had a habit of saying everything twice and often in quick succession, so sooner or later one got the gist, if not every detail, wherever one was sitting.

As the auditorium lights gradually and belatedly dimmed so all eyes focused on the tall, gangly figure as he loped about the stage, downstage right, upstage right, back to the centre, upstage left, upstage right, always on the move. Leaning forwards slightly and speaking all the time, sometimes but not always audibly, at times addressing himself to the floor and then to the upper gallery. He was a flowing river of words and here and there one picked up the odd one. 'Revolutionary,' 'never before,' 'my honour to represent Master, to be here among . . .' he spread his hands again to indicate the distinguished audience, 'I hope, I will try, I will try to do my best.'

He was riveting. There was not a person in the theatre whose attention was not now focused entirely on the tall, deranged figure of – what did he call himself? Nic – Nicholai Androvksy, Androkovsky. Assistant to the Master, to the founder of the Moscow Art Theatre – which quite possibly nobody in the audience had heard of except for Granville Barker – the man with no Christian name. Stanislavsky. Which was odd in itself, it occurred to Meredith, who knew enough about Russian theatre to know that every character had several forenames, confusingly. Stanislavsky. The Master.

Then he stopped speaking, abruptly, and stood still for the first time. He looked up. His face under the lights was pale, almost white. His features were sharply defined, almost gaunt. Sharp cheekbones and an aristocratic chin. Black eyes, to match his hair and his clothes. He stood there, hands now by his sides, for a very long moment. What an actor, thought Meredith. She would try it sometime. Talk talk talk and nobody listens. Stop dead, and you could hear a pin drop.

'I am here,' he repeated, 'to demonstrate the ways of Master, on behalf of great Stanislavsky.' His eyes ranged over the audience and came to rest, or so she believed, upon Meredith herself.

Then he began.

The Master was born of a rich family, silk merchants, he told them. One day when three years of age performing in a play to entertain the neighbours he experienced what he called a formative moment. He was given piece of wood and asked to pretend to set light to it by holding it towards a candle. So he deliberately and with what he described as 'great interest and curiosity' held the wood so close to the candle he set light to it and then to the set, which was made of cotton, as a result of which he nearly burned the house down and was consequently severely scolded. Despite this he believed his actions had meaning as the pretence did not. And this remained with him to this day and still informed his every moment on stage.

It was the beginnings of what he now referred to as his System, a series of ideas and impressions that was always changing – here Nicholai made a rolling motion with his hands – the beginnings of a System that would change the way an actor approaches his art completely. Completely.

He paused again. When he continued he began to move once more, again addressing each side of the audience in sequence. Long rehearsal times. Immersion. Absorption. That is how the system was. K S. Konstantin Sergeivich Stanislavsky. So the man had a Christian name, if not the regulatory two or three. He was a human being after all.

'We have belief, at Moscow Art. Theatre is not for money, not for profit, not for pleasing public. Theatre is . . .' he paused dramatically, 'for truth.'

He paused again for his words to sink in. The audience waited.

'Only the best, of everything. Best plays, best actors, best is all that matters. So for actors' – another gesture towards the audience – 'he has experience, of life, and this he brings on stage. The problem is, here, the actor on stage is not a person, he is actor, we know this, we do not forget it. All the time we know we are not watching real person in real life, we are watching actor. In a theatre. Artificially. This from beginning of time.'

He began his roaming again, all the while muttering and repeating his mantra of 'truth' and 'reality' and 'And so we fall into . . .' he paused again, 'cliché.' He pronounced the word precisely. 'Cli-ché,' he said again. 'This word, this word Master means to eradicate. Completely. "Cliché," he said, is what happens when actor is not present, is not thinking. It is safe place for actors. Acting is not . . .' to one side of the stage, 'it is not . . .' to the other, 'a safe place. Should not ever be.'

He was downstage now, prowling from left to right like a caged animal, his gaze roving over the front few rows of the Stalls until it came to rest, there was absolutely no doubt about it this time, on Meredith.

So when she heard the word 'volunteer' and 'demonstration' it was the most natural thing in the world for her to be on her feet before he'd even completed the sentence, before the rest of the audience knew what was going on. He nodded right at her and directed her to the stairs at the side of the stage, and before she knew it she was on it, on the very stage where . . .

Well, my word. It was the very stage upon which she had auditioned for *Mrs Morphett's Macaroons*, with Gaye Worth. It was a sign, an omen, if ever she saw one.

'Chekov.'

'Oh. Yes,' she said, slightly flustered.

'Chekov. Anton Chekov. Uncle Vanya. You know this play.' It was a statement rather than a question. As he spoke, and continued to speak, so he loped upstage to a table Merry had not before noticed upon which was a pile of scripts, picked two from the pile and loped back and handed her one of them. 'The last scene. Vanya and Sonya. So.'

There was a moment's hiatus as Nicholai looked around and scampered suddenly into the wings, to reappear a moment later with a chair, which he placed next to Meredith. As she went to sit on it, 'No no, that is for me.' He sat down - 'I am Vanya,' he said, and immediately stood up again.

'You know this play,' he said again.

'Well enough,' said Meredith.

'The family is gone. They come, and they go.' He was talking to the audience again. 'Russian countryside, Serebriakov's estate, but he and his wife, beautiful Elena, live in Moscow, many miles away. So estate is in care of Uncle Vanya, brother of his first wife, and young Sonya, daughter of same, they care for estate for Serebriakov. Serebriakov.'

He began pacing again. 'Busy man, academy man, difficult man. They come to visit the estate, Serebriakov and Elena, like important persons, and poof!' he threw his hands in the air. 'Chaos! Vanya loves Elena, the doctor loves Elena, Sonya loves the doctor. Now they are both broken. Broken-hearted. Now Serebriakov and Elena are gone, and it is just Vanya and Sonya. Alone on estate. Begin.'

He gestured at Meredith as he sat down again and spoke:

'"I am so depressed, Sonya, you cannot think how depressed I am."'

'Oh.' Meredith looked for her place in her script. 'So.'

She drew herself up to her full height, placed one hand on the back of Vanya's chair and thrust out a hip. Then as she opened her mouth to speak, Vanya – Nicholai – leapt to his feet. 'What is this?' he said.

'What is what?' said Meredith, bristling.

He placed a hand on the now vacant chair and turned to face the audience in a mirror image of Meredith's pose. 'What is this?' he said again. 'Why do you stand like this?'

'Why not?'

'You speak this to audience?'

'Well, I . . .'

'First. Loose shoulders.' He placed his hands on her shoulders and shook her like a rag doll. 'Tight. You are tight. The actor must never be tight. Always loose, as dancer.' He wiggled his body by way of demonstration and the audience tittered. 'Yes. Try.'

He stood back as Meredith, after a tiny moment, copied his movement.

'Good. Now. Again, please.'

He sat himself back down, placed his elbow on his knee and his head in his hand, while Meredith resumed her original position – hand on chair, weight on one foot, facing the audience – and began.

'"It can't be helped. Our lives must go on. And our life

will go on, Uncle Vanya. We shall live through a long succession of days and endless evenings."'

She removed her hand from the chair and sighed deeply. '"We shall bear patiently the trials fate has in store for us. We shall work for others – now and in our old age – never knowing any peace."'

She began to cry. It was a technique she had learned, she could not now remember where she'd picked it up. Very few actresses were able to cry to order and she prided herself on being one of them.

She continued to speak through her tears, first turning to Vanya/Nicholai and then away from him. She continued to speak as she traversed the stage to the far side, and as she addressed the gallery so she raised her voice, as she had learned to do under the tutelage of Herbert Beerbohm Tree.

'"When our time comes we shall die without complaining."' She mimed dabbing at her face with a handkerchief. '"In the world beyond the grave we shall say that we wept and suffered, that our lot was harsh and bitter, and God will have pity on us. God will have pity on us."'

She paused for a long moment and continued to weep silently.

'"And you and I, Uncle dear, shall behold a life which is bright and beautiful and splendid."' She walked slowly back across the stage, knelt down by his chair and delivered the next part of the speech to the dress circle. '"We shall find peace. We shall hear the angels. We shall see all the evils of this life, all our own sufferings, vanish in the flood of mercy which will fill the whole world. And then our life will be calm and gentle, sweet as a caress." Er.' She fumbled, her lips moving as she read a direction in the script, and once again she produced an imaginary handkerchief and handed it to her uncle. '"Dear Uncle Vanya, you are crying. There has been so little happiness in your life, in both our lives. But wait, Uncle Vanya. We shall find peace."' She hesitated.

'Why you stop?'

'I'm supposed . . . "We shall find peace. We shall find peace."' She paused again, and lowered her script. 'That's it.'

There came a long pause, followed by a ripple of applause from the audience. Meredith got to her feet and, turning to the audience with a broad smile and the full flourish of the leading lady she regarded herself to be, curtseyed deeply.

15: The humbling of Meredith Martin

And then all hell broke loose. Before she had a chance to curtsey again – though the applause did not strictly warrant it – Androkovski grabbed her by the arm and led her downstage and said, loudly for a change and direct to the audience: 'This is what I mean! Ladies and gentlemen! This – is – acting!'

Meredith smiled graciously. But then the warm glow that was beginning to course through her veins quickly froze.

'This is not truth! This is not reality! This is what we are trying not to do! Cliché! Lies! You!' he turned to her now, still hanging onto her arm, 'are not Sonya!'

'No? Well to tell the truth I think I am a more natural Elena,' said Meredith, with a sly smile in the audience's direction.

'Elena? You want to be Elena? Why for? You want to be spoiled, bored, self-centred woman and not warm, fierce God-loving Sonya? Pfwa!' It was a strange sound, but there was no mistaking its meaning.

'You are actress, you play as you are cast!' He was almost shouting now. 'But you must use this. This.' He was hammering his head with his free hand, the one that was not still holding onto Meredith with a grip like a vice. 'Think Sonya. Think who she is. Who is she?'

'She's Uncle Vanya's niece.'

'Yes. But who is she? She suffers! For love. You have suffered?'

It took a moment to realise he was waiting for an answer.

'Certainly I have.'

'For love?'

'Well . . .' she shrugged. She caught sight of Freddy in the third row. He was watching with interest.

'And what was the crying? What was it for?'

'I can cry to order.' She said, modestly. 'At the slightest thing. Or nothing.'

'You can cry at *nothing*?'

At last he let go of her arm and stepped back.

And then he got to work on her.

First he concentrated on 'loosening' her body. He took hold of each arm in turn and lifted it into the air and dropped it, and he continued to do so until he was satisfied she was not resisting. Then he started on her head, cupping her chin in his hand and moving it up and down, to the left to the right, round and round as if she were a mechanical doll. That done, he launched into a jig, on the spot, his knees pumping, and he gestured for her to do the same – 'Higher, higher!' He began to caper around the stage and beckoned her with him, and she never felt such a fool in her life.

And that was just the beginning.

Once the prancing was done he led her back to her spot by the chair and began kneading her shoulders again. He was rough, and she tried not to wince. It was not until he was fully satisfied that the shoulders were doing what they should be doing, or not doing, that he told her to begin the scene, exactly as she was – no holding onto chairs, no thrusting of hips. Just standing. Standing loosely. 'Is doing nothing so difficult?' he barked at one point.

She began once more, but she could barely get through a sentence before he was onto her again. What was she thinking? Where was she, was she hot or cold? What time of day was it? What could she hear? Could she hear birds? How much light? How much silence? 'No, don't tell me. Think it. Think.' He hammered at his forehead again, this time with both hands.

'Who is this woman Sonya? She is a girl, barely a girl, how old?' These were rhetorical questions, she soon realised. How long had Sonya lived on the farm? Where was she born, what did she think about? What was her day? How hard did she work, on the estate, from first light to sundown? Outside, inside, doing this, carrying that, fetching this. How hard? Alone with her uncle and ancient Marina. Alone in the big house.

She closed her eyes and allowed his voice to wash over her. She felt her heart rate slow, and then she began to do the most unlikely thing: she forgot she was standing on a stage in a theatre in front of several hundred people. She concentrated only on the voice.

They played the scene over and over, or parts of it. He interrupted constantly, repeating himself, 'Think, think. Why are you doing this? Why are you doing that? Why why why why why?' until she felt her head would burst. At the first sign of an 'attitude', whenever he spotted Meredith slipping back into her favourite and familiar posture, hip outthrust, speaking directly to the audience or the gallery or anywhere rather than to him, he would leap to his feet and forcibly push her upright. 'Look to me!' he reiterated. 'You are talking to me, to Vanya, not to them!'

As it went on she felt more and more disorientated. She'd never found acting this difficult before. She had her own mannerisms, as all actors and actresses do, and they had served her well enough. And now this. She felt she was teetering on the edge of the cliff and the ground was giving way beneath her feet.

At last they were able to move on to the end. He told her to remember a sad time in her life, with her lover, or a friend or with family. Sonya's great love, Dr Astrov, who treats her with great fondness yet like the child he believes she still is, has gone. They may not see him again. He does not love her. Elena does not love Uncle Vanya. Astrov loves Elena, or he thinks he does. It is all a sad, miserable mess. So think, bring the memory to your mind of your own time of sadness.

He was speaking more gently now. So Merry thought back to the day her father ordered her to leave the house and not return 'Until you come to your senses.' It was the first time she had allowed herself to think of it properly. The coldness in his tone, in his eyes. Her mother looking on, blank-faced. Merry hesitating, thinking he cannot mean it, he surely does not mean to throw me out. He turning on his heel and walking away, out of the hallway where this scene took place, and slowly, ever so slowly, up the stairs, step by step, not looking down.

Then that awful moment when it was just she and her mother, and her mother without looking at her or saying a word after a long moment turning and following her husband up the stairs and out of sight until it was just Meredith, alone in the middle of the hallway nonplussed, not knowing what to do next.

And now Meredith, the present-day Meredith, was fighting back tears. Crying to order was one thing, but this was not crying to order, this was real and she was not going to cry because Sonya, poor unhappy Sonya, did not cry.

'"We shall find peace."'

Sonya, who loved a man who loved someone else, whose mundane life, after a brief spell which promised hope, now lay ahead of her unchanged, with no escape, no light, nothing to break the monotony of day after day of hard, back-breaking work. Sonya, whose uncle was so unhappy he had lost all his strength and his will. Sonya did not cry because it was only she who could keep the estate going, to keep her uncle going, to find a way of getting through the days with no respite, no reward, except the reward she believed lay in heaven. No, Sonya did not cry, and therefore Meredith could not.

She swallowed, lifted her chin and said, '"We shall find peace."' And then she placed the script on the floor in front of her as if to say That's it.

There was a long pause before he spoke. 'Better,' he said.

She was exhausted. So exhausted she didn't really care what the audience made of her, of her foolishness, her capering around the stage with the mad Russian.

And not just exhausted, but oddly empty. There was nothing left in her, nothing at all. This must be what it feels like to have a breakdown, she thought. All constraints gone, all one's energy dissipated. She felt – what was the word she was looking for – free.

She scrambled to her feet, without much thought as to how she went about it. As she made her way uncertainly down the steps and back to her seat in Row C she was aware of the applause, proper applause this time. And Freddy, smiling broadly at her.

And something else: something quite unfamiliar and extremely unsettling. Mrs Vlatsky was right. She had fallen cataclysmically in love.

16: Afterwards

Before she left the stage he asked her if she would stay behind once everyone had gone so he could speak to her in private. When the theatre had emptied – Freddy offered to see her home but she smilingly refused – Nicholai jumped down into the auditorium and invited her to take tea with him in his hotel. As they walked together down Haymarket, past the theatre where Meredith had made her West End debut – what memories! – he chattered nonstop. He told her she was wonderful, a breakthrough, so receptive, so open, did she not feel it? Did she not feel the power of the Stanislavsky system? 'So simple, too simple perhaps. That is what confuses people. So difficult just to be, not to act.'

She nodded in agreement although truth to tell she was still too exhausted and dazed to really know what she thought about everything – the event itself, and now this strange, exotic man, who clutched her arm all the way as if he possessed her (which in a sense he did), steering her swiftly through the heavy traffic in Trafalgar Square until they finally reached his hotel in the Strand.

Over tea he held onto her hand across the table and, with his eyes fixed on hers – how did he learn not to blink? – he told her all about himself; how he had been born in a remote country village, the son of a blacksmith, was taken as a child by an uncle to Moscow to see a play at the Mali Theatre and it was Boom! A fiery baptism! And from then on there was only one place he wanted to be, and that was in a theatre, creating magic, transporting people, *transforming* people. By the time he got to his meeting with Stanislavsky Meredith's mind was already beginning to wander – not because she was not interested, far from it; rather that she became so absorbed with his mannerisms, the way he moved his hands, his head, the look in his eyes – so when she tried later to recall the details of his story she was disappointingly vague.

Finally he calmed down just a little, and then he took hold of her hands again and asked her if she would be his 'muse', as he put it, and accompany him on his future appearances in Scotland and other cities in the north. It was hard to believe the man who had bullied and humiliated her on stage in front of all those people was now flattering her and even, or so it seemed, seducing her over tea in a smart hotel in the Strand. She half expected him to invite her to his bedroom. And she half expected herself to agree. In the event however he merely wrote down her address and gave her a list of dates and places where he was scheduled to appear, and that appeared to be it.

At the door of the hotel he took her face in his hands and kissed her on both cheeks. He held onto her face for rather a long time while he continued to gaze into her eyes, and she waited for him to tell her Something of Moment, but instead he simply said, 'We shall see one another soon,' before turning and walking away.

~

'What are you doing?' said Mrs Vlatsky.

She had intended making straight for her room to avoid being waylaid by her landlady, but somehow

Meredith had stopped in the hallway of the house in Lambeth to stare at her face in the hallway mirror and remained there for some time.

She was looking for – what? – a change? A difference? But it was the same face that stared back at her, with some disdain, she could see it now. How odd. She had been trying out different expressions to try to soften it. Her smile, she began to think, simply made her look sardonic. She broadened it, and made it spread to her eyes, as they say you can tell a genuine smile by what the eyes are doing. That was easy enough to fake.

Was that all she was then, a fake? She had learned to smile, and to laugh, according to character and circumstance. There was the false smile, bestowed with obvious hypocrisy accompanied by condescension. That came very naturally to her. There was the smile suppressed, sometimes with the hand in front of the face, which of course was designed to draw attention to it. There was the smile coquettish, which she had deployed to great effect as the young juvenile in *An Ideal Husband*. There was even the smile genuine, often accompanied by a laugh, and she was mistress of that too, even if she was also faking it.

'Oh.' She turned from the mirror and gave Mrs Vlatsky her embarrassed smile (not totally fake). 'I was just – looking at myself.'

The lady frowned. 'Are you quite well?' she asked.

'I'm not sure that I am,' Meredith replied, which was true.

'Come and tell me what has happened.' And before Meredith had time to reply Mrs V turned away and entered her own front room, and Merry was bound to follow.

She longed to tell her landlady of the extraordinary

events of the day, she longed to tell someone. Yet how could a person like Mrs Vlatsky begin to understand what she had been through? How it felt to be asked to play a character as far from her own as it was possible to get? Sonya was a pure life force, whose heart was true through and through, there was not an unkind bone in her body. It was not a part Meredith would ever be asked to play in real life, that's to say on a proper stage to a paying audience. So what was the purpose of the exercise? Was she simply replacing one falsity with another, in order to convince the audience, or more specifically Nicholai, that she truly was the homespun, sweet-natured and above all *plain* Sonya? Come to think of it, should she not feel insulted in the first place to be asked to play someone who was by her own admission 'unbeautiful'?

Above all she did not want to give Mrs V the satisfaction of knowing that her prediction had come true.

'You look thoughtful, my dear,' said Mrs Vlatsky, as Meredith eventually followed her into her front room. 'What has happened?'

'Rather a lot, Mrs V, as a matter of fact.'

'Tell me. You have fallen in love.'

'Certainly not!'

'I think you protest too much.' Mrs Vlatsky smiled, as she lowered her large frame into an armchair and indicated for Merry to do the same. 'It was in the cards – now you must admit it, we saw it. The Queen of Hearts.'

Meredith smiled, genuinely. 'Well,' she said, and shrugged.

'It is true! This is wonderful news. You must tell me all about him.'

That was a challenge. To explain to someone like Mrs Vlatsky how she had fallen in love with a man who had spent a good hour and a half mocking, bullying and intimidating her on stage in front of a theatre-full of her fellow actors. So she gave her landlady an expurgated version of her experiences of working on stage with a disciple of the great Stanislavsky himself, of being forced to drop all her familiar mannerisms and play a simple, virginal young woman who fell in unrequited love with another man.

Mrs V hooted with laughter. 'You? You are not one to fall in unrequited love! So.' She leaned forwards in her chair. 'This man must love you back, must he not?'

'It is rather soon to assume that, Mrs Vlatsky.'

Because let's face it Nicholai had done nothing to indicate he had fallen in love with her. Having all but destroyed her he had gone on to cover her with praise and flattery, but that was all in relation to the work. What he felt about *her* was another matter. She had never before allowed herself to risk falling in unrequited love and she did not intend to do so now. She was not Sonya, not yet, not ever.

It was the cards that had done it. Those wretched cards. If someone tells you, with authority, that you are about to fall whole-heartedly in love, that very day – well, what is a woman supposed to do?

'I think he quite liked me.' Merry smiled, to herself, and to her landlady. Because never mind the cards, never mind her resistance to the very notion of love and romance and all the rest of it, when it came to it one simply had to allow things to happen.

17: The journey

Their first appearance was set for Edinburgh, which Nicholai, charmingly, pronounced with a hard 'g'. They met at King's Cross station and shared the long train journey together.

On the way Nicholai alternated between breathless garrulousness and total silence. For the first hour or so he talked non-stop about the Master. He described him as tall, imposing, and impossibly handsome, a man you could not ignore, yet at the same time a *modest* man, self-effacing even – and here Nicholai gave a rare chuckle – it was this very *modesty* that made him the great man he was. Modest and open-minded, always learning, always seeking for the truth. For new ways to find the truth and to present the truth onstage.

Meredith was entranced.

He went on to describe the workings of the Moscow Art Theatre, which had quickly begun to out-rival the long-established Mali Theatre with its reputation for experimentation and innovation. Bringing theatre into the twentieth century. A revolution in artistic endeavour, and if not to everyone's taste that was only to be expected of all revolutionary ideas. Traditions do not die overnight. But once you have seen it, have witnessed it, have stood *in the very same room* as this man . . . So it was his mission, announced Nicholai with a certain lack of modesty, to bring Stanislavsky to the world.

'Single-handedly?' Meredith interjected at one point, pointlessly.

And then he lapsed into silence for some time. He closed his eyes and appeared to sleep. And Meredith took the opportunity to study him, as he sat opposite, in repose. There was something extraordinarily distinctive about his features, the length and shape of his nose, his mouth that was both sensuous and stern. He was all angles and angularity and right now, as he slept, his body slotted into the corner between the seat and the wall of the carriage, one leg crossed over the other, as if it somehow was designed to fit whatever space it occupied. He was snoring gently.

Oh my.

Did she speak out loud? For suddenly Nicholai was awake, and alert, and he uncoiled his body and stared right at her and said, 'What are you thinking about?'

Well she certainly wasn't about to tell him *that*. So she shrugged and said, 'I am looking forward to performing at Edinburgh tonight.'

'*Performing*?' He laughed shortly. 'Ah well, yes.'

And then he went silent again, for a moment or two, and gazed out of the window. 'You are strange woman,' he said.

'Me?' She laughed as lightly as she could.

'You have quality.'

'Well, thank you.'

'No.' He held up his hand. 'Everything you do,' he spread his hands to indicate, 'is how to say, acting.'

'I don't know what you mean.'

'On stage, off stage, everything you do.'

And then he gazed at her rather mournfully, with pity

almost.

'Well,' said Meredith. 'I do not think I am alone in that. Everything we do is acting, in a sense, is it not?'

He continued to stare at her.

'Nobody is quite what they seem,' she stumbled on. 'Why, it would be a strange world if they were. Just imagine!'

'Why? Why is it necessary? You are ashamed to be who you are?'

'No, not at all. But that doesn't mean I don't like to give a certain – impression.'

'Impression? Of what? Who are you?'

For all that Meredith scorned the whole idea of small talk there were times when it had its uses.

'I am the daughter of a Brigadier.' (A remark, she was aware, that could have come straight out of Gilbert and Sullivan.)

'What is Brigadier?'

'He is a commander. In the British army. High-ranking. A notch below a Major General.'

Nicholai nodded. 'And this is what you are? An appendix – this is the word? – to father?'

'Certainly not! In fact far from it. In fact,' she swallowed, 'I am no longer his daughter, in his eyes. He threw me out.'

He raised his eyebrows. 'Brigadier threw you out?'

She nodded.

'Of what?'

'Of the house.'

'Why?'

'Because I wanted to become an actress.' She blinked away the wretched tears, she was beginning to feel like Pavlov's dog. 'The other day, in the – lecture - when you asked me to recall a sad time in my life? That is what I recalled.' She brought out a handkerchief and sniffed into it. 'The day my father threw me out of the house.'

'Because you wanted to be actress.'

'Yes. Stupid, is it not?'

'This is magnificent,' said Nicholai.

'You believe so,' she said, doubtfully.

'This is courage,' said Nicholai. 'This courage, this passion. You see? Such sacrifice. Such certainty! And for your art. This is you. This is Meredith Morris.'

'Martin.'

'The truth. Is it not?' He was leaning forwards now, his hands on his knees, his eyes gazing into hers like magnets seeking to draw out her very soul. 'So under this – ' he indicated her person, her elegant, upright person, perched upon the carriage seat in her finest, nay, her only respectable outfit of fitted jacket over tailored skirt, all of which had seen many better days, 'lies a true artist. Yes. I had thought so.'

He leant back in his seat again but continued to scrutinise her.

'I didn't think he really meant it, not at first.' She was sounding, she realised to her annoyance, rather childish. 'And I did think he would change his mind. That perhaps, one day, when I was established, he would come to his senses. That one day there he would be, at the stage door, my mother by his side, and he would take me in his arms and . . .' Now she was being fanciful. Her father had never taken her in his arms, not ever. Nor, come to think of it, had she ever up until this moment truly harboured the dream she was describing, the reconciliation. But now she'd started she could not stop. 'That is why it is so important for me to become established. Do you see?'

'And this is why you are actress? For someone else?'

'No. And then again, yes, in a way. If you mean did I

109

become an actress to impress my father? Certainly not.'

He nodded. He was still gazing at her.

'All actresses want to impress other people, do they not? Is that not the purpose of acting in the first place?'

'To *impress*?' He leaned forwards again. 'What is impress?'

'To please. To amuse other people. So they admire you. Think well of you.' She cocked her head to one side.

'Why do you want to "impress"? How do you do this if you are not yourself?'

It was getting altogether too metaphysical for words. With anyone else Meredith would have done something to end the conversation decisively. But Nicholai was not anyone else.

'If you are only what you want people to think you are,' said Nicholai, 'you are not truthful. If you are not truthful you are not actress. Cannot be.'

'I don't believe that is necessarily so,' said Meredith. 'When one takes on a role one becomes someone else.' She wanted to ask what "truth" had to do with anything when one was playing the part of a flibbertigibbet in *An Ideal Husband*. But then she had never actually played Chekov on stage. Or Ibsen, come to that.

She wondered if the stuffy old world of Edwardian England was quite ready for the likes of Stanislavsky and his emissary Nicholai and their "truth". If they already found the New Order of Granville Barker mildly shocking what would they make of revolutionary ideas emanating in a country like Russia?

Never mind. It was thrilling nonetheless.

The conversation seemed to end there. Nicholai folded his body back into his seat and closed his eyes again.

There will be more, thought Meredith, contentedly. More conversations. More of everything.

18: Touring the truth

The Edinburgh masterclass was quite different. Of course, nobody in Nicholai's world wanted to repeat himself.

He talked about the ethos of the Moscow Art Theatre under the leadership of Stanislavsky. How it worked as a complete entity, like a machine, all the parts moving together, without friction, and with one simple ideal, which was not to make money or success or reputation. The ideal of Stanislavsky's Moscow Art Theatre was to make the best work to the highest standard. For this, Nicholai explained, with emphasis, they are led by Art, by what Art tells them. And so they attract best actors, and actors stay for a long time, and every actor in Russia wants to work at Moscow Art Theatre. Every actor. Not for one play, not for one season, but for all time.

She recognised in Nicholai's description the ethos of Granville Barker at the Court Theatre: the insistence on company rather than 'stars', the apparent disregard for commercial success, the emphasis on the repertory system; and like the Moscow Theatre the Court did attract the best actors and even the best actors worked better there than they did elsewhere. So there was clearly something in all this.

In these thoughts, she was aware, Meredith was

probably alone. The audience around her were quiet, and apparently baffled. When she was invited onto the stage she felt an atmosphere that was not quite anticipatory, not quite engaged. She rather imagined there were few if any actors among them and they had no idea what they were watching.

Nicholai threw a quite different scene at her, of course. It was again from *Uncle Vanya* and again she was to play Sonya. It was a scene between Sonya and Elena, Sonya's stepmother, the beautiful young woman desired by both Uncle Vanya and Dr Astrov. When Sonya confides in Elena her love for the doctor the reaction of the other woman (played, rather incongruously, by Nicholai) is unexpected.

'"I've loved him for six years,"' Sonya confesses. '"I love him more than I loved my own mother. And now you're here he comes every day, but he doesn't look at me, he doesn't even see me. It's breaking my heart."'

'"Does he know?"' asks Elena.

'"No. He doesn't even notice me."'

This was a quite different Sonya to the Sonya who comforted her distraught uncle at the end of the play, who showed such strength and purpose and a glowing belief in the afterlife. This was a pleading Sonya, a pathetic, self-pitying, deluded Sonya. This was not a woman Meredith was able to empathise with on any level.

'"I tell you what,"' says Elena, '"I will talk to him. It can't be too hard to find out whether he loves you or not. I'll be discreet. We need only to know if it's a yes or a no. What do you think?"'

At which point Sonya is supposed to look terrified and miserable and excited all at once, which was even more of a stretch for Meredith. But she was on stage, there was an audience, and there was the Master's emissary, whom above all else she wanted to impress – no, to please – no, to obey . . . Gracious me, how does a woman impress a man who does not even understand the notion of being impressed?

Finding the 'truth' in this Sonya was a proper challenge. There was nothing in Meredith's experience that she could dredge up to represent the violent emotions Sonya was required to express. If one were looking for truth, to be frank, Meredith's truth was nothing other than scorn for the girl's stupidity.

It was the very point Nicholai picked up on immediately.

'What is she thinking, Sonya?' he demanded.

'She's thinking her whole world depends on whether or not the doctor loves her.'

'Yes,' he said. 'Yet she says he barely notices her. He only comes to visit to see Elena. So why does Sonya think he can love her?'

'I've no idea,' said Meredith.

This was a mistake.

'You must have idea!' He raised his voice. 'You are Sonya! You are not Meredith. I do not want Meredith's idea, I want Sonya's!'

'Then I . . .' she stumbled, and recovered quickly. She was on stage after all, in front of all those people.

'She is deluded,' she said.

'Sonya, deluded? Yet Sonya is practical woman. Clear-minded, sensible woman. And she truly believes the doctor loves her? How can this be?'

'When it comes to love, common sense has very little to do with it.' She was tempted to add, 'So I have been told,' but didn't.

'Continue.'

'When it comes to love . . .' she stopped. The fact was,

in certain aspects she felt distinctly superior to Sonya. There was no way Meredith would allow herself to fall in love with someone who did not love her back. Her self-respect would never allow it.

'Sonya is a very passionate woman,' she said. 'With very strong feelings. And she is spontaneous, and open-hearted. She loves easily, and whole-heartedly, without inhibition. She has not yet learned to hide her feelings.'

'Yes?' He was standing so close to her she could feel his breath on her face.

'Of course she knows the doctor does not love her, because she is plain, she says so herself, and naïve. And yet she believes he could. She knows she can save him from his own self-disgust, that she has the strength to revitalise him, to rebuild his faith in the world – this is the strong Sonya, the unselfish Sonya. She may look pathetic, yes, and yet it's the practical side of her who believes he could grow to love her, if only he would allow her to love him and nurture him.'

She was unsure where these thoughts were coming from, but they were beginning to make a kind of sense to her. As she spoke she saw Nicholai's shoulders begin to relax, and she even thought she saw the hint of a smile on his face, and when he spoke he did so gently.

'Good,' he said. 'Now show us.'

And she did. This time there was less bullying and humiliation, there was less need for it. He had her repeating moments, speeches and parts of speeches, over and over until he felt satisfied it was Sonya he was working with and not Meredith.

And in the end, somehow, she triumphed. By the end of the session she was Sonya, her heart bursting with love for a man she truly believed could love her back. And then the world would be a better place, and she would fill it with love, and care and comfort the broken, disillusioned man she knew she could restore to health and happiness. For that was what Sonya was placed on earth to do: to love and to comfort and to heal, if only she was allowed to. For this brief period of time Meredith felt she had stepped into Sonya's shoes to the extent that she was the gawky, plain young woman who had never loved or been loved by a man; who needed, yearned, hankered for the feel of a man's arms around her, holding her, caressing her, being transformed by her.

It was not so hard after all. In place of Dr Astrov there was Nicholai, on whose affection and approval Meredith depended more than she cared to admit. Sonya may never have the chance to love and transform the doctor but on this occasion she had well and truly transformed Meredith.

It was extraordinary. In losing herself and becoming someone else Meredith was, she felt for the first time, understanding what it meant to be a proper actress.

~

The audience response when it was all over was muted. Nicholai was morose. It took some doing to convince him this was due more to Edinburgh reticence than a lack of appreciation or engagement. Meredith utilised her newfound affinity with Sonya to reassure him, to comfort him. She even tried to place an arm around him but he shook it off.

She was tempted to ask him - What does the audience reaction matter? According to his own stated description of the Moscow Art Theatre the audience was of minimal importance, was it not? But Nicholai was not so much despondent as angry, 'They did not listen.'

'They did listen. But they may not have understood.'

'Then they are stupid.'

'That's as may be. But isn't it up to the person on stage to make things understandable?'

He grunted.

They were walking together back to the hotel. Meredith tried at one point to take hold of Nicholai's hand, just as he had done with hers the first time they met, but he was having none of it. He had descended into his own private world, an angry world.

'They were not actors, Nicholai,' she said, gently, as if to a child. 'I believe they were attentive, very attentive, and thoughtful. Perhaps more thoughtful than the London audience. Anyway,' she drew a deep breath. 'What does it matter what the audience thinks? Isn't that what they teach at your Moscow Theatre?'

He stopped there, in the middle of the pavement, and gave her a look to freeze a desert.

'You too.' He shook his head and carried on walking.

When they reached the hotel they ascended the stairs together to the first floor in silence. At the door to Meredith's room they stopped, and she took his hand as she opened the door and pulled him firmly inside and he did not resist.

She laid him gently down upon the bed and then she removed her shoes and lay down beside him. She shuffled closer and reached over to stroke his cheek. He turned onto his side and flung a languid arm across her, and she held onto that and positioned herself so her face was all but touching his, ready for the inevitable kiss. At which point he closed his eyes and fell immediately fast asleep.

Oh what a tangled web! Meredith turned onto her back and gazed at the ceiling. So near and yet . . .

She had done well that evening, on stage, she knew she had, and so what if the audience didn't completely follow what was happening? She thought she was due some gratitude, or at least an acknowledgment of what she had put herself through in order to serve Nicholai's purpose.

He began to snore, right there on the bed next to her. The ultimate insult.

She could not help but laugh.

19: The Manchester miracle

If one does, as Meredith believed people did, choose to be a particular sort of person in one's life, and it turned out that person was neither admired nor particularly liked, one might have to reconsider one's choices, even at the not so tender age of twenty-five.

She had developed a grudging admiration for Sonya. The fictional young woman created by a middle-aged Russian man had grown from a pathetic, ugly – her own description – unsophisticated country bumpkin into something almost noble. Sonya had a firmer idea of who she was than Meredith herself. But then Meredith was an actress and Sonya was not.

She pondered these things over breakfast the following day. She had woken up the previous evening – she was not aware of having fallen asleep in the first place – to find Nicholai gone. She had spent the remainder of the evening on her own. At dinner in the hotel dining room there was no sign of him, and now he appeared to be skipping breakfast. She half wondered, not without alarm, if he had left the hotel completely, without a word of goodbye or thanks.

What did he think of her talent? That's what she really wanted to know. If anyone were to disappear without a by-your-leave it should surely be her, the woman who allowed herself to be exhibited in front of a theatre-full of bewildered customers, to be experimented on like a living dummy.

But that was the old Meredith talking. The Meredith to whom dignity and respect were paramount. If she were to relax her shoulders, as she now knew how to do, might the rest of her follow? Was it too late to turn oneself around? In Life as in Art was it all too easy to fall back on old habits?

'Good morning,' he said, as he took the seat opposite her. He whipped the napkin off the table and onto his lap and buried his face in the menu. Everything he did was done with precision, and intensity; at this particular moment the menu was the only existing thing in the world.

'Did you sleep well?' she asked politely.

'Yes.' He closed the menu and placed it back down on the table, folded his hands together and looked at her. 'Yesterday you were good,' he said. 'Yesterday you were Sonya. This is quite remarkable.'

'Why, thank you.' She found herself almost blushing.

'It is the System. It proves System works. If you, Meredith Morris, can follow System.'

'Martin.'

'Gestures, voice, all. From this . . .' he thrust out his chest and raised one arm in the air in a ridiculous parody of Meredith's acting, 'to this.' He lowered his arm and sat simply. 'It is good.'

She swallowed her natural indignation. Instead she said, humbly almost, 'I felt a little like Sonya. A lot like Sonya. In the end. To tell the truth.'

'Yes,' he said. And then, to a hovering waiter. 'Coffee, no milk. Bread roll, jam, no butter.'

The waiter nodded and departed.

'Which is surprising,' she went on. 'Because I am not Sonya, I could not be more unlike her. I didn't even like her, not to begin with. But then I suppose an actress does not necessarily have to like the character she is playing. Well?'

'Hmm?' he said. His thoughts, clearly, were elsewhere.

'Tell me something Nicholai.' She took a deep breath. 'Do you think I am a good actress?'

'Good? Good student, yes.'

'Yes, but am I good at the acting too?'

He looked at her as if he had no idea what she was talking about.

'I do need to know. Because in this world, in this business, you know, with all the rivalry and so forth, it is very hard to know whether one is . . . or whether one might be more successful . . . why one is not as successful as one should be.' She tailed off completely.

Nicholai stared at her for a moment longer before the waiter appeared with his coffee and bread roll.

His hands. She watched as he poured his coffee. She studied his fingers on the coffee cup. Long, thin and delicate, like his face, like his body. He was a contradiction. A tyrant's mind inside the body of an angel.

That was the end of that conversation. And of course there was no way Meredith could bring up the subject again.

~

Manchester was an altogether different experience. To begin with the audience comprised a hefty component of schoolchildren, who had no hesitation in jeering or cheering at random moments, not all of which had to do with what was happening on stage.

This time it was a scene between Sonya and Astrov in which Sonya expresses her admiration for him.

'"You are so different from everyone else I know,"' she tells him. '"You're a fine man. So why ever should you want to be like ordinary people, the sort who drink and play cards?"'

This drew the odd jeer from the audience.

Sonya implores the doctor not to drink so much and he appears to comply. '"I'll stop drinking right away. You see? I am now quite sober and I shall remain sober for the rest of my days."'

He goes on to say how old he feels, old and dejected, tired and second-rate. And then Sonya asks him the all-important question.

'"Suppose I had a younger sister,"' says Sonya/Meredith. '"Or a friend. And you found out that she loved you. What would you do?"'

'"Younger sister? What younger sister?"' says Astrov/Nicholai. He doesn't get it. He just shrugs his shoulders and tells her he would do nothing, he has too many other things to think about. Then he shakes her hand rather abruptly and leaves, to jeers, and cheers, from the stalls.

By this time Meredith had grasped, without having to be told, that she should begin the performance as her old self, her old, gesticulating, acting self, in order to give Nicholai something to work on. And work on her he did, with his usual vigour, and she resisted his instruction, and objected, and asked him over and over to explain himself, as she had now learned to do, until she appeared suddenly to see the light. At which point the transformation of Meredith into Sonya began to take place before the baffled eyes of the youngsters in the audience. And when it came to it, the scene was finally performed in complete silence.

After it was all over a lady appeared at the stage door

asking to speak to Mr Androkovsky. She was, she explained, a teacher, and she had been very much alarmed at what she and more particularly her young charges had just witnessed.

'What am I supposed to tell them?' she demanded. 'That it's acceptable for a man to treat a lady with such rudeness?'

It was at this point that Meredith arrived on the scene. She found the lady in full flow and an open-mouthed Nicholai so far failing to interject a word.

'Not in my lifetime,' she babbled on, 'did I see such a thing. And you a foreigner to boot, you should be ashamed!'

'And what does being a foreigner have to do with it, may I ask?' Merry almost barked at the lady.

'You!' The woman turned to Meredith and took a step back in surprise. 'How do you let this happen to you?' Then, leaning towards her and confidentially taking hold of her arm she said, *sotto voce*, 'Is he oppressing you? You can tell me, Miss Morris – it is Miss Morris, is it not?'

'It's Martin, as a matter of fact. And you are?'

'My name is Miss Sylvia Blithe, deputy head mistress at St Catherine's Upper School.' With which she thrust out a hand which Meredith took and hung onto while she said:

'Miss Blithe, let me explain. What you saw this afternoon was a demonstration of the System of Stanislavsky, who as Mr Androkovsky told us has revolutionary ideas about theatre and performance. What we were trying to show on stage this afternoon is how an actress of the old school can be transformed into someone altogether more believable, more truthful, even when – especially when – the character she is playing is quite unlike herself.'

She let go of the lady's hand and threw a quick glance

across to Nicholai before continuing.

'Your concern is understandable, laudable even. But if you were able to explain to your pupils that what they witnessed this afternoon was not real life, that it was a *demonstration*, then perhaps they might understand it all in a different light. You see,' she carried on before the lady could interrupt, 'I was before a very bad actress, all gestures and posturing, concerned only with how I was coming across onstage and giving almost *no thought at all* to the character I was playing. Then this gentleman,' with a gesture to the still speechless Nicholai, 'came along and put me right. It took some doing. All that harrying and bullying, it was necessary, believe me, to jolt me out of my old habits and rethink everything. Habits are very hard to break and sometimes it requires shall we say extreme methods to make one look at things afresh. Do you see?'

Miss Blithe stared and said nothing.

'I owe everything to this gentleman.' She tucked her arm into Nicholai's proprietorially. 'It is my privilege to be his pupil, to be given first-hand knowledge of the great Stanislavsky, who in times to come will become a household name, believe me.' That was a stretch, but never mind. 'He has transformed me as an actress. And as a person,' she added for good measure.

She held onto Nicholai's arm throughout but she tried not to look at him. For as she was speaking she realised she had finally become Sonya completely. In expressing her admiration for his teachings she was also expressing her love for the teacher. Whether or not Nicholai was aware of this, or had any inclination to reciprocate, was another matter.

20: Virginia

If one were to step outside one's surroundings and observe them from afar, which is not something Virginia was generally prone to do, much of one's daily activities looked pretty pointless.

On the other hand respect was also due to the people who gave point and purpose to every activity, however apparently inconsequential. Conversation was one. Much of it, especially in social occasions such as parties and dinners, was naturally trivial. 'Naturally' meaning it was understood among certain classes that conversation was a fluid thing that could be easily interrupted or terminated as one switched one's attention from one person to another. It was an unspoken rule that one should *never* monopolise another person nor embark upon a topic that could be regarded as even mildly contentious.

So it was that Virginia found herself observing the room she was in, which was filled with men and women all beautifully dressed and all apparently utterly and totally engaged in what looked like lively conversation. The absorption was admirable. Regardless of their content these conversations held a much more important purpose: they made people feel that they *mattered*. The non-talkers, that's to say the listeners, had mastered the art of appearing to listen even if their minds were most likely elsewhere: head on one side, now frowning now laughing, their attention evidently focused totally on the speaker so that only the most acute observer would notice the odd flicker of an eye over the other person's shoulder to see if there might be better entertainment available elsewhere.

Virginia laughed out loud. Or rather she would have done had she not been brought up to suppress every spontaneous thought that came into her head.

She was, she admitted to herself, bored. Usually she would have joined in, she would be the one with her head on one side appearing to pay attention to her chattering companion. She'd spent years being a devoted listener and now, frankly, she'd had enough.

At the same time she was also envious of the people, women especially, who seemed so content to spend an entire evening talking about topics such as the latest scandal involving the monarch, French fashion or the Perennial Problem of Servants. Why should these women be concerned with something like female suffrage? A good majority of them ruled the roost in their households anyway. Why waste their time demanding the vote when they had it already? Mrs Pankhurst may not have appreciated this incontrovertible fact, being a widow herself of course.

But what of the rest? The traditional wives, the likes of Virginia Stephenson, who took their cue from their spouses and 'knew their place'?

She was reminded of a conversation she once had with her old friend Nesta Hastings. Nesta, who was married to an Oxford don and lived in a cottage in Hampstead with an unruly garden and a sign on the front door saying 'Beware of the cat' – which she swore kept the pigeons away even though they did not own a cat – had left school at fourteen and was largely self-taught, and now she spent her days writing books about Plantagenet monarchs 'for fun', as she put it.

'You are very much a pair, aren't you?' she ventured to Virginia over lunch one day. 'You and Maurice. Never a contradictory remark, even though he does come out with the most astonishing stuff on occasion, I hope you don't mind my saying. I admire your loyalty, I really do.'

'What exactly are you referring to, Nesta?' Virginia enquired, with a smile.

'Oh, all sorts of things. The British in India, that's one. I suppose it's the army upbringing, they don't see the Empire crumbling all around them.'

'Is it?'

'We're all living in the past, more or less, at our age. University professors not least. At graduation the other day – the procession of dons gets longer and longer and older and older, I swear some of them have been dead for half a decade and they just disinter them from time to time. And there they are, covered in cobwebs, can barely make it down the aisle. It's the only time anyone sees them all year.' She laughed. 'But that's by the way. Anyone with an iota of sense could see all Empires are doomed, you only have to look into the past. A country marches uninvited into another country and forces its language and its religion and its education onto the poor inhabitants, and then surprise surprise, those poor inhabitants decide due to their newfound education that they can handle things on their own, thank you very much.'

'You think that's how Maurice sees things?'

'You tell me, Ginnie.'

She could not immediately think of a reply.

'You've never really thought about it, of course not, why should you? A lot of women depend on their menfolk to do their thinking for them.'

That stung. It was true and of course she knew it was true, which is why it stung.

Virginia's brief foray into politics, and civil – or at least domestic – disobedience when she attended the suffragette rally seemed like a long-ago memory. It was thrilling to have been in the thick of an event that had reached the front pages of the newspapers, to be in her own small way doing Something of Significance in this world. And it had given her ridiculously childish pleasure to have defied her husband.

But since then she had slipped back into her old world, and it dismayed her. She had tasted the forbidden fruit and she wanted more of it.

She was beginning to see her daughter in a different light. Meredith had done it. She had ploughed her own furrow and sacrificed her family for it. At the time it had seemed very different. To Virginia, if not to Maurice, their daughter's defiance had seemed like a rejection of everything they had ever done for her, a slap in the face in return for years of nurturing and education to make her the person she was. Did she not love them? That is how it had looked to Meredith's mother at the time: her daughter did not love her, and therefore it was right she should be banned from the house until she saw the error of her ways.

It shamed her now to think she could have been so stupidly simplistic. Meredith's behaviour had nothing to do with love, or the lack of it. It had to do with a young woman following her passion – a passion that she, Virginia, starkly lacked. She had to face the fact that she envied her daughter.

It was time she got off my backside and did something, Virginia resolved. What that 'something' might be was to be worked out in the future. But right now she knew exactly what she wanted to do first.

21: ADA

Following the showdown with the schoolteacher the relationship between Nicholai Androkovsky and Meredith Martin was consummated decisively and enthusiastically in their hotel that same night. It transpired that Nicholai could be surprisingly playful as well as passionate, and throughout it all he spoke to Merry in Russian, which raised the level of her eroticism to heights never before experienced in the sexual history of the world.

So this was what all the fuss was about, Meredith thought. Well, fancy. I owe a lot of people an apology. It was a form of madness, this love business, but what glorious madness! How bright the world looks when you are in love! How sharp, how vivid, it was almost violent, this sudden awakening, this feeling of living for the first time. Darling Gaye, I understand you now.

Sober up, you fool, she told herself. The world is no different today than yesterday. And yet nothing was the same nor would ever be the same again.

~

The following day Nicholai told Meredith about an experiment the Master tried back in Moscow, where he would dress as a tramp and wander the streets, talking to other tramps in order to understand them.

'Now we could do the same,' he suggested. 'Here, on the streets. You as Sonya, I as Astrov. We walk on the streets as Sonya and Astrov, into restaurants, everywhere we are Astrov and Sonya, not Nicholai and Meredith. We try.'

'You mean we go out and about in character,' said Meredith.

'Strictly. All the time. What happens, we react as Astrov, not Nicholai. A person speaks to us, we respond as Astrov, or Sonya. What do you think?'

'I think it's a splendid idea,' said Meredith. I will follow you to the ends of the earth, as Sonya or Meredith or anyone you wish me to be, she did not say.

And so they spent the morning wandering the streets of Manchester, talking as the two characters in *Uncle Vanya* might do. Meredith placed her arm in Nicholai's – or Astrov's – as she told him how wonderful he was and how much she admired a person who devoted his life to others. And how satisfying to know that you are contributing to the world and will leave your mark upon it.

'Do not talk that way,' said Nicholai/Astrov.

'Why not? It is true.'

'It means nothing.'

It wasn't always clear if it was Nicholai talking or Astrov. Nonetheless on she went, about how dull and pointless life could often seem if you have no satisfying work to do. She felt truly sorry for Elena, no matter how beautiful she was. She had always been envious of beautiful people before, as a woman who was not.

Here she paused, and waited.

'She is beautiful,' said Nicholai/Astrov. 'She is most beautiful woman on earth.'

It was not quite what Meredith was hoping for.

'People should not be judged on their outsides, they should be judged on what goes on in here.' She touched her chest with her free hand. 'Anyway, beauty doesn't last.'

'Is this Sonya or Meredith?'

It went on like that for a while – Meredith/Sonya doing most of the talking and Nicholai/Astrov interjecting now and again.

The *piéce de resistance* took place in a restaurant over lunch. In order to start up a conversation with a stranger Meredith began to regale the waiter with the astonishing qualities of her luncheon companion, who she explained was not only a doctor but who owned a large estate in the country that he was fighting to protect from intrusion from outside, and how he knew more about trees than anyone else in the entire world. As the waiter, smiling nervously, slowly backed away from the table his side of the conversation was taken up by a ruddy-faced man on a nearby table who claimed that he too was a farmer and he would be very interested to hear her companion's views on what was happening to the birch trees, which on his land he thought were showing signs of some "foreign disease".

Nicholai, with a calmness that quite took Meredith by surprise, listened patiently to the stranger and then announced that yes, it was quite possible his birch trees had developed a disease, most trees did from time to time, it was very difficult to eradicate them. The best advice he could offer was to prune the diseased trees right back to the trunk and wait to see what happened.

'It's good advice,' said Meredith, taking hold of Nicholai's hand. 'He really does know everything.'

The farmer nodded, only partly convinced, and resumed his lunch.

'He's also a doctor,' Meredith persisted. 'He treats everyone. It doesn't matter if they have money or not, if there is ever anyone in need, he will be there.'

'Really?' piped up a strident female voice from across the room. 'How very interesting. Please may we have your details, doctor?'

Nicholai removed his hand from Meredith's and barked, 'I do not live here, madam, I am sorry I cannot help you.'

'Oh,' said the lady. 'I thought I heard you talking about your country estate. I assumed you lived nearby. Although,' she sniggered to her companion, 'anyone with a country estate around here could well afford not to charge for his services.'

Meredith took a firm hold of Nicholai's hand again. 'We live in Russia,' she explained to the lady across the room. 'In the middle of nowhere.'

'Oh,' the lady exclaimed. 'Well, that's most inconvenient.'

'I apologise, madam,' said Nicholai. 'Another time I would be happy to help.'

Afterwards, as they strolled back to their hotel they laughed about it together. 'Who would have thought?' cried Meredith. 'For one moment I imagined she might threaten to follow us back to Russia.'

'This is true,' said Nicholai. 'But you, Sonya, she is too – ' he hunted for the word, 'too exaggerant, is that the word?'

'What do you mean?'

'"Oh, he is so clever, with this, with that, a doctor who understands trees, who cures people, anybody he will cure, for no payment."'

'It's true,' said Meredith.

'It was *silly*.' He pronounced the word with emphasis,

as if happy to have thought of it. 'Sonya was not silly.'

'Oh. Well, I'm sorry I'm sure. But I think it's exactly the sort of thing Sonya would have said to a stranger. Given the chance. It's part of her naivety, if you like.'

He grunted.

'Whereas I, Meredith Martin, would not dream of doing such a thing. I would have felt utterly foolish, telling the world all about you. Sonya on the other hand is precisely the sort of girl who could land a person in hot water through her sheer enthusiasm, just as it happened in the restaurant. She wants the whole world to know what a wonderful man you are.'

She turned to look at him closely. 'Do you not agree, doctor?' she said, and they both laughed.

She felt oddly, and gloriously, liberated.

~

From Manchester they travelled back to London for Nicholai's final engagement and checked in together as Mr and Mrs Androkovsky at a small and suitably discreet hotel in a side street off Leicester Square, where their liaison continued unabated. 'On honeymoon?' winked the receptionist as they finally emerged from their bedroom on the third day of their stay. To which Meredith responded, with uncharacteristic civility, 'How did you possibly guess?'

Nicholai's final engagement took place at ADA, the newly-formed Academy of Dramatic Art, founded by none other than Herbert Tree in the Dome of Her (now His) Majesty's Theatre and now occupying a tall and slightly shabby building in Gower Street. (Tree, whom Meredith informed her lover she had once known well, though not *that* well, while no longer in sole charge of the Academy was immensely proud of it and insisted his name be recorded on all Academy printed material as

'Founded by H B Tree in 1905'.)

The former Meredith might well have sneered at this shabbiness as she followed her lover up the endless stairs to the not-terribly-large room at the top, where a group of eager students sat awaiting their arrival with eager grins on their fresh young faces.

That there should be such a thing as an Academy to teach people how to act would have been in itself suspect to the old Meredith. Old Meredith always claimed everything she had learned about acting she had learned 'on the job', and no thanks to ex thespian Willard Featherbridge. But New Meredith was curious, even slightly jealous of these excitable young students. Post-Sonya Meredith was prepared to give the place the benefit of the doubt, especially bearing in mind the almost overwhelmingly enthusiastic welcome they received at the hands of the Academy's administrator, the genial and handsome George Pleydell Bancroft (son of the well-known actor-manager Squire Bancroft and his wife Marie) and his staff, which comprised a group of equally eager-faced women and men who lined up like guests at a ball to greet Nicholai and his companion as if they were royalty.

Having seated Meredith in the front row right next to ADA's principal Nicholai began his presentation. This time he approached things rather differently. He sat himself down on a chair onstage and addressed the students in a confidential tone about what he referred to as the Art of Acting. It was not a Craft, he explained, or even a Skill; to call it anything less than Art was to demean the Noble History of Drama reaching back to the Ancient Greeks. Anyone seriously considering a profession in the Noble Art should consider themselves Privileged and Obliged, among a Chosen Few who had elected to take on the Mantle of Drama and devote their lives to the perfection of it.

No one else in the world could have spoken such words and made them sound not just comprehensible but inspiring, thought Meredith. Speaking in his halting English, at conversation level, Nicholai was at his most mesmerising. His audience were all but falling off the edges of their seats with awe.

He described the beginnings of the Moscow Art Theatre and its founder Master Stanislavsky's philosophy of Art for Art's sake, that any other consideration such as pleasing an audience or making money destroyed the purity of Art. The audience listened in total silence, nodding now and again and in time ever more vehemently until the young softly-spoken Russian had the entire room in the palm of his hand.

The Master was not a natural actor, Nicholai explained. He struggled, physically and mentally, with awkwardness and self-consciousness. There were times when he did not know what to do with himself on stage: how to move, how to stand, how to hold his head, how to perform the simplest action, none of it came instinctively to Maestro Stanislavsky. So he began to work on himself, and *this* – and here Nicholai paused dramatically – is why he has become the great teacher he is.

He then called Meredith onto the makeshift stage, where once again under his dogged and painstaking instruction she went through her by now well-rehearsed transformation from old-fashioned Poseur to living and breathing Sonya. She was aware this time that she was demonstrating exactly the experiences of the Master himself; that original Meredith was every bit as self-conscious and 'unnatural' as original Stanislavsky. As a compliment to herself it was double-edged, you could say.

The effect, in front of these closely-engaged students,

was remarkable. There were one or two open mouths as Meredith stepped off the stage to a round of applause that, while nothing compared with the audience of a theatre in London or Manchester (or even Edinburgh), did its best to take the roof off the tall building in Gower Street.

Having finished with Meredith and Sonya, after a short interval Nicholai spent the second half of his class working on the students themselves. He was, by his standards, relatively gentle with them, if every bit as thorough and persistent. One poor Sonya was almost reduced to tears by his constant interruptions, his insistence on repeating a scene or a speech over and over until at last she reached what he regarded as the Truth. The overall standard of acting talent was, in Meredith's view, somewhat wanting. She even imagined offering her services as a teacher – part-time of course – while she pursued her own acting career.

Ah, but then. Was she going to be available? After all she would, she supposed, be living in Russia in the future, with Nicholai, working at the Moscow Art Theatre with the Master himself. Not right away, of course not. She would have to learn the language first, but with Nicholai's help surely it would not be long before she would be taken on as part of the Company. And as Nicholai liked to make clear, very clear, once a member of the Company always a member of the Company.

She could perhaps make the odd trip back to England now and again to give masterclasses on the Stanislavsky system with Nicholai, along the lines of the Trees and the Bancrofts only far, *far* more progressive.

Once it was all over and the students had dispersed Mr Bancroft turned to Nicholai and immediately offered him a position at the Academy as a part-time teacher. And for that all-too-brief moment between the offer and Nicholai's response Meredith had conjured up yet another scenario, this time based in London in professional and personal partnership with Stanislavsky's right-hand man, running a theatre together – perhaps the Court itself –specialising in Russian plays, often in the original language, featuring the renowned actress Meredith Martin and demonstrating the by-now well-known Stanislavsky System. From time to time they would travel to Europe and perhaps to America to make guest appearances . . .

'Thank you, but it is impossible,' Nicholai replied to Bancroft. He smiled. 'My life and my heart is in Moscow.'

So that was that. Ah well, Russia it was then.

~

Mrs Vlatsky's reaction to Meredith's announcement was predictable.

'You go to live in *Russia*?' she exclaimed. '*Forever*?'

'I would never say anything is forever,' said Meredith calmly. 'There is always a possibility we will go to live elsewhere at some point. But Nicholai is very much attached to his theatre in Moscow, you see, and indeed to the Master himself. And who am I to stand in his way?' She smiled sweetly.

'No!' cried the good lady. 'This cannot be!'

'You always wanted to see me married off, Mrs Vlatsky. You could even say it was your doing.'

'*My* doing??'

'The cards. It was you who told me I was going to meet the man of my dreams on that day, don't you remember? Clever you. I never doubted you, you know.'

'But . . .' Mrs V gestured wildly. 'This . . . I never thought . . . What am I going to tell your mama?'

'My what?'

'Your . . .' Mrs V stopped dead, and clamped her mouth shut, and stared furiously into the fireplace.

'What do you mean, what are you going to tell my mama?' She spoke evenly, even calmly, for this was the new Meredith, the humble-yet-confident Meredith. And when the good lady did not reply she reached over to her and took hold of her hand and said ever so gently, 'Mrs Vlatsky, speak to me. What did you mean?'

At last Mrs V looked up, and to Meredith surprise and dismay there were tears in the lady's eyes and her mouth was turned down like a small child's.

'It doesn't matter,' she croaked. 'I did not mean anything.'

'I think perhaps you did. Tell me.' Still she spoke softly and still she kept hold of the lady's hand. 'I will understand, I promise you.'

And so it came out, the whole story. How Meredith's mother had paid a surprise visit to the house in Lambeth a few years earlier when Meredith was appearing in *Mrs Morphett's Macaroons* and had asked, or begged Mrs Vlatsky in return for small gifts of money – very small, which she accepted in place of rent when Meredith was not working because she, Mrs Vlatsky, had come to look upon Meredith as her own daughter – to write to Mrs Stephenson from time to time with news of her daughter's well-being. And while it had pained Mrs V to do so as she so despised secrecy, and it was never her intention to deceive, or to betray, Mrs Stephenson was so insistent, and so upset, and she so loved her daughter, truly, and it was for her that she did it – for Meredith, cried the lady – because one day, she hoped and prayed she would see mother and daughter reunited. And it was for that reason alone.

When she stopped speaking Meredith let go of the lady's hand and stood up and walked slowly to the fireplace, where she remained for some time, motionless.

Finally she turned and smiled and said, still with the gentle calmness of the New Meredith, 'Well thank you for your concern, Mrs Vlatsky. But be assured I shall be removing my things by the end of the week and after that you will never see me again.'

At which, with a brisk flick of her skirt, she was gone.

22: The best-laid plans

On her way back to the small hotel in a side street off Leicester Square Meredith planned her conversation with Nicholai, which went like this:

> She: If you decided to stay in London rather than return to Russia we could hire a theatre together and you could introduce the theatre world to Stanislavsky directly. We could form a company and produce Russian plays – like an offshoot of the Moscow Art Theatre. I could introduce you to the most influential people in English theatre such as Herbert Tree and Granville Barker – now there's a man after your own heart, he would love to learn the Stanislavsky system. We would be the toast of London town. What do you think?
>
> He: It is a possibility. I could invite the Master over at some point, to direct a play.
>
> She: Oh, better and better. And I would become the most celebrated and respected actress in London and then my father would come knocking at the stage door and beg for forgiveness!

That was perhaps a step too far. In truth, if her other dream could be fulfilled she cared not a jot what her parents thought of her. There was still a bit of Old Meredith left.

'He has checked out,' said the hotel receptionist as he handed Meredith her key.

'Who has?' she asked, stupidly.

'Mr Andro – Androkovsky. He asked me to tell you.' He was the same young man who had made that cheeky remark about honeymoons, only this time he was not meeting her eye.

'I don't understand.'

'That is all I know.' She may have been mistaken but she thought she caught the beginnings of a smirk on the young man's face.

'What about a message? He left a message, surely?'

'Not that I know of. The room is paid for tonight only.' He coughed into his hand.

It wasn't, it couldn't be a mistake. Yet it had to be. As she made her way stiffly to the room on the second floor Meredith puzzled, and speculated. Surely there would be a message inside the room, he had made no indication, not the slightest sign, the last time she saw him. Why of course, it was understood once the last class had finished, he would be making his way back to Moscow eventually, but . . .

She hunted. The bed was made up, the towels folded neatly, her clothes were still in the wardrobe, but of a message there was no sign. Vainly she looked inside the bed, beneath the mattress, inside the dressing table drawers, on top of the wardrobe. Hidden. He was teasing. There had to be something somewhere.

There was not.

She sat on the bed and remained there for an entire hour without moving.

Ship. She could find out which shipping line he used, there can't have been many operating ships to Russia. But where to begin?

P & O, she'd heard of them. It was the only line she had heard of. She could start there, it shouldn't be so difficult to locate their London office, and besides how many passenger ships sailed from London to Moscow in a week? Was Moscow on the coast? He could have gone to another city in Russia. Or indeed anywhere else. He could be stopping off on the way. For all she knew he was not sailing back to Russia directly, he could be making more guest appearances in other countries – France perhaps, or Italy. Or America. Or.

It was useless. A useless quest.

There are some things in life a girl never learns.

Damn him. Damn Nicholai and damn his stupid Stanislavsky system and damn men in general and above all, damn Mrs Vlatsky for getting her into this situation in the first place and for allowing her, Meredith Martin, the one with a head on her shoulders, to lose it. To lose all sense of proportion and common sense. Old Meredith would have seen this coming. Old Meredith would have crossed the street, done anything to avoid getting herself into this utter mess. Old Meredith, the person she was so eager to put behind her, turned out to be right about things after all. New Meredith would have to expunge herself and the entire past six months from her brain and her memory.

She lay back on the pillows and tried to sleep.

What would Sonya do? Spurned by the only man she had ever loved, her unchanging future stretching out before her like a long and empty road with no escape, Sonya kept going. Thanks to her faith in God and her strength, her extraordinary belief in – what? – the glory of suffering? Or the hope of redemption in a world to come? Is that what Sonya felt? What a fool she was if that was the case.

He had simply used her, as a model, a doll, in his theatrical demonstrations. The rest – the sex, the affection (come to think of it did he ever really show her real affection?), were just distractions. He had toyed with her. And his final cowardice, to disappear without so much as a note, a goodbye or a reasoning, not just showed him to be a total good-for-nothing it was a blow to her pride and her discernment. Worst of all he had turned her into that most wretched of clichés, the spurned woman.

She was a living (barely), breathing (with difficulty) Sonya.

It was not until the early hours of the morning that sleep, that saviour of souls, finally interrupted her self-lacerations. She slept until the chambermaid appeared at her bedside well into the following day apologetically explaining they needed her to vacate the room.

She left the hotel without aim, without direction. She had no home. She had no work. She had no money. Things were, all in all, looking pretty bleak.

There was only one person she could turn to.

~

All things considered Gaye seemed not too displeased to see her old friend. 'All things' being the fact that she had set neither eyes nor ears on Meredith for quite some time, since before the baby was born, and now here she was, on her doorstep, in trouble. A fair weather friend indeed.

It had taken a while for Merry to track Gaye down. She had moved from her one room in the Mile End Road to a small apartment in a street nearby – the current tenant of her old room was not sure of the number – and it took a knock on several doors in that same street before Gaye eventually answered.

'Coming up in the world,' she announced cheerily. 'Slowly.'

She had the baby in her arms and was looking exhausted. The baby was – well, who was to know how old it was? – it was a baby, that crawled, and chattered to itself in a language that made no sense to anyone except its mother, who appeared to dote on it and find it the funniest thing on two legs – or rather two knees, as the legs had yet to be drafted into commission. It was, said Gaye, a terrible sleeper and yet it had all this energy and never stopped from dawn to dusk, and she couldn't remember the last time she had a good night's sleep. But she wouldn't change anything, not for the world. It was the light of her life, and so clever, and *really* good company, and bla bla bla, and by now Meredith had stopped listening.

But yes, said Gaye, there was the sofa, if Merry was that desperate, and she sure looked it. As a temporary thing anyway. And she could look after the baby now and again and give Gaye a breather. That would be useful. For now at least.

The idea of looking after the baby – who was female, it transpired, and named Claudine – was not appealing. But Merry was a beggar and not in a position to choose. And while the apartment was not that much bigger than the proverbial shoe box it was cosy enough, and cluttered in the cheerfully chaotic way that accompanies all families with small babies and no servants to clean up or protect the adults from their progenies. She even got used to the horsehair sofa that was her bed, where she spent the nights trying to ignore the lumps and all thought of the creatures that no doubt inhabited it, and resisting the urge to cry.

There was little opportunity for Meredith to tell Gaye her story, or indeed to talk about anything much with the baby around. Not only did it use up all its mother's energy, it – she – also managed to monopolise the conversation.

'They do take you over,' said Gaye, unnecessarily. 'It's hard to think about anything else.'

'How is Billy?' Meredith ventured.

It seemed Claudine's father's progress towards his first fortune was proceeding slowly, yet steadily, her mother insisted. He now owned several stalls on Petticoat Lane and another somewhere in Bermondsey, which he let out to others for a fee which brought in a small but regular income. Enough to keep them in nappies, his wife giggled.

Those same nappies, once used, were placed in a pot on the stove, where they appeared to sit for hours, or even days, boiling away until they were not just clean but almost threadbare. As for the changing of them, this was an experience Meredith managed to avoid completely until one day when the smell became overpowering and she was compelled to negotiate the perilous combination of soiled nappy, safety pins and wriggling baby. She found it helpful to sing loudly as she did it, largely because it involved breathing out rather than in.

It all helped to take her mind off her predicament. When Gaye was out, which she tended to be increasingly as the days wore on, and it was just Merry and Claudie, as she was known, it was a full-time job simply keeping a hawk's eye on the small creature as she pelted on all fours from room to room, at random, with no particular purpose it seemed other than to find Interesting Objects to place in her mouth. From time to time she would stop dead and gaze at Meredith and break into a toothy grin, which came dangerously close to melting Merry's heart.

She wondered what might be going through the baby's head. There was certainly something. Here was a tiny person, too young to understand words, or to mimic, or to do anything other than exactly as she wanted whenever she wanted to do it, without thought or hindrance, guidance or instruction. To learn how to eat, how to suck, how to crawl, all without being told. To scream when she felt like it if things were not to her pleasure; to be the centre of attention of anyone who was present, to be coddled and cuddled by both parents equally. Who could not envy such a creature? Who would not wish she could stay this way forever, to preserve her from the needless anxieties that awaited her in the adult world? From now on, thought Meredith, all this little thing has to look forward to is Repression and Refusal. No, you cannot eat that carpet tack. No, you cannot crawl through the front door to be mown down by a passing carriage, or eat lollies all day, or stay up until midnight, or go out without your parents knowing your whereabouts, or fraternise with unsuitable people, or choose a profession your father disapproves of or make a fool of yourself over a man who clearly has no feelings for you whatsoever.

'Best stay as you are, little Claudie,' said Meredith.

23: Mrs Stephenson pays another visit

It felt far easier this time round. This time it was not a deception it was the ending of one. And how very much simpler it is to be truthful, thought Virginia, not for the first time, as she gazed out upon the river from the top deck of the 'bus crossing Lambeth Bridge.

She was ready for rejection. She was under no illusion that her wilful daughter, having been so cruelly and peremptorily discarded all those years ago would come running home again with her tail between her legs and a grateful smile on her face. She quite expected Meredith to refuse to see her. All she wanted was the opportunity to come clean, to apologise, and see what happened. The rest was up to Meredith.

Mrs Vlatsky greeted her at the door in surprise and some distress. Her eyebrows were crinkled with anxiety and, so Virginia noticed for the first time, very nearly met in the middle.

'I'm sorry to land upon you without warning.' Mrs Stephenson gave the lady a reassuring smile as she stepped across the threshold of the house in Lambeth and made her way uninvited to the front room. 'But that was deliberate. I have decided,' she announced as she removed her gloves and sat down, 'to make a clean breast of everything. With Meredith. It's utterly ridiculous. To tell her she can come home any time she likes.'

Mrs Vlatsky took a seat very gingerly in a chair across the table from her uninvited guest and gave her a nervous smile.

'Is she in? It doesn't matter if she refuses to see me, that's quite understandable.'

Still Mrs V appeared tongue-tied.

'Well?'

'No,' said Mrs Vlatsky abruptly.

'No, she's not in? Well that's perfectly all right, you can pass on a message to her. Do you happen to know where she is? No, don't answer that, it's not my business. Well?' She repeated.

'She has gone,' said Mrs Vlatsky.

'Gone where?'

'To Russia.'

'To . . . Oh. Well now. Does that have something to do with the – that – what was his name? The one she was doing those – what do you call them, classes? Demonstrations? – you told me something about them, I never did quite grasp what that was all about.'

Mrs Vlatsky nodded.

'So she's gone to Russia with . . .'

'Nicholai.'

'Nicholai, was that his name?' She thought for a tiny moment. 'On what basis? I mean, professional or personal? Or perhaps both? I have to say I did not expect that.'

'She has gone for good.' The lady was almost whispering. She brought out a handkerchief and began to rub it between her hands. 'To work, and to . . .'

'For good? How can that possibly be? She doesn't speak Russian! Or does she?'

It was an awful lot to take in. She had known, as Mrs

Vlatsky had told her, that Meredith had been touring the country with a Russian man teaching some kind of acting method, and that – and this was Mrs V speculating, she made clear – there might have been an attraction between them, as she, Mrs V, had predicted from the cards. But now to just up sticks and take off to a foreign country where the people – why, who knows what the people were like in Russia, she rather fancied they were semi-peasants who lived in the dark ages and drank vodka in the daytime, and wasn't the weather in winter too awful for words? What on earth could induce her headstrong, fiercely independent daughter to sacrifice her ambitions to do such a thing?

Just then Mrs Vlatsky began to cry, and Meredith's mother found herself comforting a woman she barely knew because her own daughter had left her.

'There there, Mrs Vlatsky, she will be back, I'm sure she will.'

Mrs V shook her head vehemently. 'No.' She sniffed into her handkerchief. 'She said no, she would never see me again. She was very, very angry, Mrs Stephenson. So angry.'

'Angry? With whom? With you? Why should she be angry with you?'

She began to know the answer to this as she asked the question.

'Ah. She knew.'

Mrs V blew her nose loudly. 'I was – when she told me, I was very upset. She has come to be a daughter to me, Mrs Stephenson, like my own daughter, especially as . . .'

'As her own mother had abandoned her.' Virginia nodded sadly.

'And I said something – I do not recall the words – I thought, she is going to live in Russia, with this Nicholai, and her mother does not know, how can she do this, and how can I tell her mother? These things I thought, I did not say, not out loud. Yet she guessed, somehow. So I told her everything, I thought, if she is going to live in another country, it must . . . she must be told. She – was – so – so angry. So angry.' She banged the hand that held the handkerchief on the table in front of her as she spoke. 'Not with you. With me. For the lies, the pretend. And I . . .' She sniffed again. 'I hate to pretend, I did not intend – I don't know how it came to all of this.' She spread her hands helplessly. 'All of this.'

It was an odd situation, even Virginia had to appreciate that. She reached out to take the hand of the crying woman, the hand that still held the by now rather damp handkerchief.

And then she did an odd thing, she began to laugh. Mrs Vlatsky looked at her in alarm.

'I'm sorry Mrs Vlatsky, please forgive me.'

'She went without taking her things,' Mrs Vlatsky spoke rapidly, nervously, as if to a madwoman. 'She said she would come back to take them, but she did not. By now she will be in Russia. And she did not take her things.'

'Well, that's neither here nor there.'

'I have kept her room for her.'

Virginia nodded.

'She always came back. I kept her room for her because she did not otherwise have a home.'

'You have been very good to her, Mrs Vlatsky, I really appreciate it. And I hope she did too.'

'No. She did not. Not in the end. In the end she . . .' Mrs Vlatsky began to cry again.

Virginia sighed. 'What a God-awful, unholy mess,' she said.

She took her time making her way home. She walked aimlessly through the side streets of Lambeth across Kennington Lane to Lambeth Palace and on to the river. She felt oddly detached.

It was the end of something, something that could have been so easily avoided. She was as much upset – more, possibly – for Mrs Vlatsky as she was for herself. Mrs Vlatsky had been nothing but kindness itself, a wholly innocent, put-upon, exploited woman whom she, Virginia, had coerced into being party to a Grand Deception.

That her daughter was lost to her forever there could be no doubt at all. Had she timed it better, before all this Russian business, she might, just might have been able to salvage something. As it was, there was a kind of justice to it all. She, Virginia, had got exactly what she deserved. That Mrs Vlatsky had become unwittingly involved in it all was unfortunate. She would make it up to the poor woman somehow, she had no idea how.

As for Maurice. Her first instinct was to tell her husband his daughter had been run over by a 'bus and was now lying fatally injured in St Thomas's Hospital, the very building she was walking past right now.

That made her laugh again. When was it, she asked herself, that her instinctive reaction to any difficult situation had been to lie? Was that what her life had come to?

It was not until she was safely home at St Leonard's Terrace and had told her maid Martha that no, she did not need any refreshment thank you, she was going upstairs for a rest and did not want to be disturbed, and she had climbed the three floors to her bedroom until she was well out of earshot of anyone, that she allowed herself to lie down on her bed and sob her heart out.

24: Coming up for air

Anyone who had ever known Gaye's father would not have been in the least surprised to hear him give his daughter a hard time the moment she gave birth.

Born – as he claimed she was – in the dressing room of a music hall in between shows her parents were appearing in it was to be expected that Gaye would not let something like the arrival of a small baby make any difference to her professional life. That Gaye herself had been longing for an excuse to take a break from working was not something Jimmy Worth would have either understood or, given the chance, allowed. That there was another man in his daughter's life who held more sway over her than her father was neither here nor there in his eyes. What was both here, and now, was the 'squalor' in which his daughter was living with husband, baby and it seems for the time being her erstwhile friend; which meant that if Billy Tilling couldn't summon the wherewithal to provide his family with decent premises it was his wife's obvious duty to do her bit.

All this Gaye told to Meredith as the arrival of her mother and father at the rooms in Mile End gave them both the opportunity for a break. The café in which they now sat, inappropriately named the Paradise, while nowhere near on a par with their old haunts in Piccadilly was for Gaye a home from home, somewhere she escaped to, with the baby, when the loneliness and oppression of those two rooms became too much. She was on first-name terms with the waiters and waitresses, they knew her likes and dislikes, they even on occasion when the boss wasn't looking refused to take payment for her hot chocolates and her iced buns, both of which had been added to the menu at Gaye's request.

The two women, once working partners, one-time allies and serial rivals, had a lot to say to one another. It seemed as if the release from those two murky rooms had given them permission to talk freely, about everything and everyone. Of course she loved her baby, said Gaye, more than she ever believed anyone could love another thing, and she didn't miss the boards at all – not *that much* Merry, she said, holding up her finger and thumb with barely a gap between them – and she loved her husband too, she really did. It was just that, how could she put it? There had to be more to life. Somewhere. And no, going back to the music hall, as her father had insisted, was not the answer. It had to be somewhere else, wherever life was hiding. She wanted to travel. To go to exotic places where everything was different. Where there was no routine, no day was like any other day. Where the sun shone all day long and everything was weird, and strange, and, well, exotic.

Meredith harrumphed, and said something about there being no such thing as total happiness, wasn't life about looking for things? Always wanting what you don't have, even if you don't know what it is you don't have? In her case it had been quite straightforward, focused even, she knew just what she wanted and she went for it. She really went for it. And now look what happened.

'What did happen?' asked Gaye with her mouth full of iced bun.

So at last she began to describe to her friend the bare bones of her experiences with Nicholai, and as she did so and since it was the first time she'd been able to talk about the whole sorry business, which in past weeks she had so successfully pushed to the back of her mind, she found herself putting skin on the bones and telling everything, forcing back the tears as she did so. The more she spoke the more foolish it sounded and the less like Meredith: considered, upright, practical Meredith, who never cried at weddings (except for Gaye's) and scorned all forms of romantic sentimentality.

Gaye's expression, as she listened for once without interruption, veered from pity to scepticism and back again, with some surprise thrown in.

'It sounds foolish when I tell it like that.'

'It does,' Gaye agreed.

'I never would have thought.'

'Nor me,' said Gaye.

'I always had an eye, an inkling, you know? For what was genuine and what not. I mean you have to, don't you, in this business?'

'True enough.'

'But this time, I don't know what happened. It was a mixture of – it wasn't just personal, you know? It was what he did. To me. And no, I'm not talking about the bedroom, you can wipe that smile off your face right now, Gaye Worth. I'm talking about on stage. What happened between us on stage.'

'He taught you how to act.'

'Or not to act.'

'About time,' said Gaye.

'And that's the difference. Because I felt like an utterly different person Gigi, do you get that? Do I seem to you like an utterly different person?'

Gaye considered her friend for a long moment.

'Yes and no.' She sipped her hot chocolate. 'When I see you with Claudie I'm quite surprised.'

'What do you mean?'

'You seem almost like a human being, you know? You forget yourself when you're with Claudie. You never used to do that, that's for sure.'

'What are you saying?'

'You were never off duty, if you get my meaning. More than anyone. Us actresses tend to be, you know, not ourselves. We're so used to having to be what we think someone wants us to be.'

'Not me.'

'Especially you. Only you didn't know it. As if you was on stage all the time, being looked at, being judged. I used to wonder what you'd be like when there was no one around, just you alone, and I bet you was no different.'

Meredith studied her plate.

'And you got worse. Since you decided to call yourself "Meredith", as if "Merry" was too silly, you thought people didn't take you seriously. Worse than that. You thought it mattered if people didn't take you seriously. Honest to goodness.'

'That's probably true,' Meredith acknowledged.

'Now you've made a whopping fool of yourself – best thing that can happen to a person.'

'How can you say that?'

'It's true! You admitted it yourself. You made a fool of yourself. Which only goes to show.'

'Show what?'

Gaye shrugged. 'That you're not so different from the rest of us after all.'

There wasn't much to say to that.

'And now,' Gaye leaned across the table towards

Meredith, 'you can call yourself a proper actress. You owe him that much, Nico – whatever you call him.'

'I paid a big enough price.'

They sank into silence for a while.

'I still can't . . .' Meredith began.

'Can't what?'

She shook her head. 'Well I'm usually . . .' She stopped. 'The cards. That's what began it all. I really don't think if it hadn't been for the cards . . .'

And now she was compelled to explain them, how they worked, how she believed they worked. Most importantly, why she believed in them.

'They were always right,' said Merry. She looked up and across the room, which at that time of the afternoon was largely, and thankfully, empty. 'They knew about me, or she did, Mrs Vlatsky, she seemed to know all about me without my telling her. That had to be the cards, or so I thought.' She switched her gaze to her friend. 'Don't laugh.'

'I'm not laughing.'

'And it turned out the reason she knew about me was nothing to do with the cards, it was because my mother, my own mother . . .' she paused, and blinked back the tears, 'had actually been to the house when she knew I wouldn't be there and had made this – arrangement. With my landlady. So Mrs Vlatsky was writing secret letters to her all these years, and I had no idea.'

There was a pause.

'What's wrong with that?' asked Gaye.

'What's *wrong with that?*' Meredith shook with irritation. 'My own mother, and my landlady, were deceiving me all along, both of them.'

'And that's why you left.'

Meredith nodded.

'Doesn't seem much of a reason to me,' said Gaye.

'Well then you understand nothing.'

'That's probably right.'

There was a long silence. Merry nursed the cup that held the tea she had not drunk. Then she said, 'I did once think I'd ask you round so Mrs Vlatsky could read the cards for you.'

'Then why didn't you?'

'I thought . . .' She was trying not to smile. 'I was afraid of what she might say. About you and Billy.'

'You was afraid she might tell me I was making a whopping mistake.'

'I was afraid she'd say quite the opposite. That you were all set for a glowing future.'

Gaye frowned, and then she smiled, and nodded. 'I get it. You didn't want me to be happy because you didn't think you could get along without me.'

'If you want to read it that way.'

The waiters were all leaning up against the counters, deep in conversation. They might just as well have been all alone in the Paradise Café at half past three on a Wednesday afternoon.

'So you did believe in them once.'

'The cards? I did, truly. They predicted *Mrs Morphett* as a matter of fact. And they predicted Nicholai. That's when the rot set in.'

She described how her landlady had gone into paroxysms that morning at the sight of the Queen of Hearts.

'Meaning?'

'Meaning I was going to meet someone special, obviously.'

'Hmm.' Gaye toyed with her teaspoon. 'And did she say it was going to be Nicholai?'

'Not by name, of course not.'

'But you knew it was him.'

'How do you mean?'

'Was there no one else there that day? At the theatre?'

'No. Well, yes, obviously. There was a whole audience. Hundreds. Maybe a couple of hundreds.'

'That's a lot of someones.'

'What, you mean I got the wrong person?' Meredith laughed, rather hysterically, and loudly enough to make the waiters momentarily cease their conversation to turn and stare across the room at them.

'Who else was there? Anyone you knew?'

'I can't remember offhand.'

'Who you were sitting next to, say?'

'What, you mean – Freddy? Freddy!' Meredith laughed again until her shoulders heaved. 'Not Freddy. Absolutely not.'

'Why not Freddy?'

'Because he's a fool,' said Meredith.

~

There was a tramp who regularly stood at the corner of Gaye's street and the Mile End Road, which is why on exiting the house Merry would make a long detour in order to avoid walking past him.

Old Meredith would have barely noticed him and would simply have walked on by. Old Meredith had been brought up, like so many of her time and background, to view the poor as at the least invisible and at most as another species, who had brought their own poverty on themselves by their idleness or their ignorance, or both. There was a joke the brigadier was fond of telling, that if you gave the working classes baths they would simply fill them with coal. It made him laugh uproariously every time he told it.

But now this same tramp, who appeared cheery enough, with his broken-toothed grin and his chirpy 'Spare us a penny or two, lady', Meredith found positively threatening. Right now there was very little to choose between them. Her upper-class upbringing had hitherto protected her against the likes of him. But woe betide the person who eschews her background and thinks she can survive without its embedded attitudes or the protection of its prejudices.

What a strange old life it is, she mused as she automatically took the long route – turning left out of the house to the end of her street, turning right and then right again in order to find herself far enough down the Mile End Road for safety – that both Gaye and I have defied our fathers: she by refusing to go back onto the boards and I by insisting on treading them. She did not regret this decision, not for one moment, though had she at the time foreseen its consequences . . . Well, sometimes it's best not to be able to see into the future.

However for some reason on this day, on impulse, Merry decided to double-back and, reaching into her purse she pulled out a whole shilling and dropped it into the tramp's hat. A shilling she could barely afford. His response was fleeting, almost casual. 'Ta very much, lady,' he said, and effectively dismissed her from his presence.

She hesitated. She very much wanted to talk to him, to find out more about him and his life. If only the social gap between them weren't so utterly unbridgeable. How could a person like Meredith hope to have any kind of a conversation with a tramp without sounding either patronising or obsequious?

There was no question about it, it had been far easier being Old Meredith, with her certainties and her assumptions. Despite everything, Old Meredith no longer existed. What existed in her place was not quite New Meredith but someone between the two, a person Merry had yet to fully discover.

~

It was not long after their visit to the Paradise Café that Gaye was taken on there as a waitress. She took Claudine with her and kept her in a small playpen behind the counter, and such was the camaraderie at the Paradise that the staff took it in turns to play with her and to feed or comfort her when she became restless. It didn't pay much, or so Merry assumed, and it was a far cry from Gaye's dream of a new life in some far-away fairyland, but in every other way it was ideal for Gaye. It got her out of the house and in congenial company, and the burden – as that is how Merry saw it – of looking after the baby twenty-four hours a day was considerably reduced by being shared. Claudie was happy, Gaye was happy, Billy was happy, Gaye's father shrugged his shoulders and muttered something about it being 'better than nothing I suppose'.

It left Merry out on a limb of course. But in any case it was time for her to be moving on.

25: Moving on

She found herself a cheap hotel off Euston Road. On the first evening she sat down to write to George Bancroft at ADA offering her services as a part-time teacher of the Stanislavsky system. He wrote politely back, thanking her for her offer and explaining that at the moment he was fully-staffed but that he would keep her details close to hand. And meanwhile should she hear that Mr Androkovsky was planning another visit to London to please tell him he would be delighted to hear from him.

She then sat down to write a ten-page letter to Nicholai, in which she expressed her dismay that a man who built his life around the Truth should be so fearful of it when it came to his personal life. She doubted that a man who was so obviously devoid of any sense of decency or humanity should ever amount to anything, professionally or personally. And while she wished him well in his role as assistant to the Master Stanislavsky she could not rid herself of the belief that in the end he would be found to have feet of clay, and that he would be banished to Outer Siberia and spend the rest of his life in hard labour, whatever that entailed. And finally that she was considering writing directly to The Master to warn him of his assistant before he was able to do any more damage.

She tore the letter up.

She then wrote to Stanislavsky himself telling him the whole sorry story of Nicholai's exploits in England and advising him to divest himself of his protégé at the soonest opportunity before he could cause too much damage. She tore that letter up too.

Her desire for revenge was all-consuming.

She had postcards printed announcing herself as an "Actress of the West End and teacher of the famous Stanislavsky system of the Moscow Art Theatre", available for teaching or performing positions, which she arranged to be placed in shop windows in Kensington and Chelsea. Two weeks later she was contacted by the Principal of the Roehampton Academy for Girls, based confusingly in Gloucester Road, inviting her to be interviewed for a part-time position teaching Elocution, Deportment and Genteel Manners. The interview was brief, so much so she barely had a chance to mention her skills as a teacher of Stanislavsky, and she was engaged on the spot. Since the term had already begun she assumed she was filling an unexpected vacancy and that she was hired not so much for her skills as a teacher of young ladies as for her general appearance and above all for her voice.

There was no immediately obvious way to incorporate the teachings of Stanislavsky into a class for Elocution, Deportment and Genteel Manners. She experimented, inviting the young ladies to combine walking around the room with books on their heads in the character of a duchess, say, or an acrobat or a Hungarian princess. It was all done for fun and her pupils, being the submissive young ladies they'd been brought up to be, took it in good part.

It all helped to keep the wolf from the door.

Although, literally speaking, it didn't. When another guest at the hotel, whom she believed to be known as Mr

Hannay, insisted yet again on knocking on her door in the early hours of the morning in the belief that she was A Lady of the Night, and yet again she was dragged from her bed to assure him, in her best SW3 tones, that she Was Nothing of the Sort, she decided enough was enough. The following day she packed her meagre belongings and caught a cab to the house in Lambeth.

~

Mrs Vlatsky was surprisingly unsurprised to see Meredith. It was almost as if she had been expecting her. Of course, she would be back to collect her things, and of course they were still there, as was her room, waiting for her, as ever.

She asked no questions, but her soulful expression expressed her sympathy. She simply shook her head and said, 'I never liked Russia. It's too cold.'

'The whole world has been asking for you,' she told Merry, as she poured tea.

'Such as who?' enquired Merry.

'Oh, everybody. Mr Symonds . . .'

'Bertie? What did he want?'

Mrs V shrugged. 'There was an actor, a young actor who said he had worked with you. And a Miss Robinson, or Robins. She wrote you a letter. I told them all you were in Russia.'

Mrs V opened a drawer in her corner whatnot and pulled out a bundle of letters tied together with ribbon. 'Here.'

Meredith riffled through them. There were a couple of letters from fellow actors saying nothing in particular, wondering how she was getting on, including a chunky missive from her erstwhile onstage companion Freddy Prentice, which she placed in her bag to read later. There was a note from the producer of the Oscar Wilde play she had previously toured with offering her another tour (this time in a comedy called 'The Merry Widows of Winchelsea'. With her newfound talents as an Actress and a Person of Truth the days when Meredith could be seen in such frippery were well and truly over). There was a neatly written letter from Elizabeth Robins inviting Meredith to the inaugural meeting of the Actress' Franchise League in December – 'Have I really been gone that long?' Merry wondered out loud. There were a few scribbled notes from actresses and fellow suffragettes about the same topic.

'Nothing from my mother?' she asked.

Mrs V shook her head.

'Has she visited here? Since – you know . . .'

'Since you walked out in a tempest?' Mrs Vlatsky smiled. 'As a matter of fact, yes. I told her you had gone to Russia for an indefinite time.'

'Oh. How did she take it?'

Mrs Vlatsky shrugged. 'She was upset. As was I.'

Merry nodded.

'She seemed to think Russia was full of peasants who drank vodka all day long. And that it was freezing cold for most of the year, which is true. In fact, she was the comfort to me.' Mrs Vlatsky sniffed. 'I was upset also, you understand. We both were. We both were a comfort to each other.'

'I am sorry, Mrs Vlatsky, deeply sorry.'

'She thanked me for being a better mother, as she put it, a better mother than her real mother.'

'That is true, actually.'

'No.' Mrs Vlatsky dabbed at her eyes. 'Your mother is a good woman. She loves you. As do I.'

'Oh, please Mrs V, don't get me started.' Meredith laughed to mask her tears.

'You – are – 'she jabbed at Meredith with her forefinger, 'a very lucky woman, Meredith Martin.'

'Merry,' said Meredith.

'Merry?'

'Yes. From now on I am Merry. In name if not in nature.'

Mrs Vlatsky stared at Merry for a moment, and then shook her head again.

'I know,' said Merry gently. 'I am a lucky woman. To tell the truth I don't feel particularly lucky at the moment, but I am. I will be.'

They drank their tea in thoughtful silence for a moment. Then:

'So are you still in league with my mother, Mrs V?'

'I beg your pardon?'

'The little – arrangement that you had with her. Where you reported back to her on my wellbeing, as you put it.'

'Of course not. She thinks you are in Russia.'

'Hmm.'

'And I shall not – I do not intend to inform her this is not the case.'

Mrs V stared sternly at the younger woman, who shifted her gaze to the floor.

'Thank you,' said Merry.

As she got up to leave the room she said, 'You know Mrs Vlatsky, your cards were entirely wrong.'

'How you say this?'

'Your Queen of Hearts. That day. That was what led me on the path to . . .' Merry shrugged. 'I so believed in your prediction. I am not sure if it hadn't been for the cards, well, I'd have kept my head. I usually do keep my head, as you know.'

Mrs Vlatsky frowned. 'The cards are never wrong,' she said gravely.

~

It was a couple of days before she got round to reading

Freddy's letter. She turned it over a few times in her hand, wondering how he could have contrived so many jokes and riddles to fill up several pages.

The letter began, predictably, with a riddle. Or what appeared to be a riddle.

'What happened to the lady who bared her soul before two hundred and fifty people?' He went on to say that since he learned she had gone to Russia chances were this letter would never reach her, therefore he could say what he liked.

As she read so her attention was caught, and she shifted from a bored slouch to sitting upright in her chair. She read the pages through, paused for a long thoughtful moment, then read them through again. Finally she stood up and, still clutching the pages to her, she went to the window and stood there for a considerable time, looking out.

26: Bertie again

They met at the Salisbury public house in St Martin's Lane which, as was immediately obvious to Merry as they stepped through the door, was frequented by many 'Bertie-likes', a good deal of whom he knew.

'Forgive me if I don't introduce you dearie,' he said as they threaded their way through the crowds. 'It would take all evening. Now sit yourself down and tell me things.'

They found a free table in the corner and while Merry settled herself he bought them a bottle of wine. Once their glasses were filled and "chin-chinned", and Bertie had wriggled his backside into the unforgiving leather of his seat, he thrust out his chin and said, 'It's been a very long time, you naughty woman.'

Merry was momentarily distracted by the surrounding clientele. There were aspects of London she knew nothing about, she realised.

'What is this place, Bertie?' she whispered.

'It's called the Salisbury, my dear, named after a Prime Minister or other. And there's no need to whisper, we're all friends in here.'

'That's what I mean.'

'And so far none of us is doing anything illegal, though that could change at any moment.' He winked at her and drank some wine.

'It's –' Merry gestured widely, 'wonderful. I had no idea.'

'There's no reason why you should. But when you are forced to lead an underground life you find ways and means. And places. It isn't difficult. There are plenty of us.'

How odd it was, she thought, that so many people – not just men, she surmised from the present clientele – found themselves on the wrong side of the law for simply being who they were.

'But how do you know? How do you pass on messages, and so forth?'

'It's very simple. We have an underground railway. And an underground language, with codes and so forth. You get to know your way around. Though to tell the truth,' he took a large sip of his wine, 'it can get shall we say a touch claustrophobic, not to say inward-looking. That's why it's good to introduce a fresh face now and again.' He gestured at Merry's glass. 'You're not drinking your wine.'

'Are there women as well?'

'As in . . . why yes, of course.'

He jerked his chin at a huddle of people at the bar. It contained several recognisable faces, of both sexes.

'Well, fancy.'

'Fancy indeed. You'd better buck up, dear child, or there will be little left for you.' Bertie refilled his glass. 'The irony is,' he continued, 'if it didn't have to be quite so underhand we would not obsess about it quite so much.' He took another deep drink and sighed. 'It gets extremely tedious, believe me. If you want to make something boring, and mundane, so boring and mundane that nobody wants to talk about it, legalise it.'

Merry toyed with her glass before drinking. 'That would be a shame, in a way,' she said. 'Not so much fun I think.'

'It depends on which side of the fence you're sitting.' At which Bertie all but snatched Merry's glass from her and held it to her lips. 'What's the matter with you, you used to be able to keep up.'

Merry laughed, took the glass from him and drank. 'I am a new woman, Bertie, can't you see it?'

'Don't tell me you're a teetotaller. I will have nothing to talk to you about.'

'No, not like that.' Merry sighed, and once again toyed with her glass as she surveyed their surroundings. It was a surprisingly elegant pub, she realised, all beautifully-carved wooden panels and glittering coloured glass. Though why she should be surprised at its elegance perhaps showed her own narrow-mindedness.

She took another drink before, on Bertie's insistence, she launched into her story: her first meeting with the notorious Nicholai (she tried to keep the venom from her voice, at least to begin with) and her introduction to the Stanislavsky system. She tried to describe his revolutionary acting method of Searching for the Truth and how, under Nicholai's instruction, she had demonstrated how it worked, not just once, but several times, in front of eager – or relatively eager – paying audiences. Of the effect this had had on Meredith as a performer and as a person, and how the whole experience had opened her eyes to her own failings, as an actress and to some extent as a person. How from now on she was to be known, as she used to be known, as Merry rather than Meredith (which really had little to do with Stanislavsky or Nicholai), and that if she could not be given the opportunity to demonstrate the Stanislavsky system in performance, on stage, in an actual play, then she would become a teacher. That she had, in fact, begun teaching already and was thinking of opening up her own Academy, in prestigious premises somewhere in London, her own London version of the Moscow Art Theatre. Right now she was considering possible titles for the Academy and would welcome any suggestions.

She went quiet then, and drank her wine, and turned to gaze around her.

'Was that all that happened, dearest?'

'No,' she replied sharply. 'But that is all I want to talk about. What do you think, Bertie?'

'Of your Truthful Method? I can't say it sounds appealing.'

'But it's high time, don't you agree? The theatre has become altogether too artificial for words.' She could have been spouting Oscar Wilde. Bertie burst out laughing.

'My dear, well demonstrated. I'm sure you're right. But if theatre holds a mirror up to life, isn't that precisely what it should be?' He shifted in his seat, and chuckled. 'If you are really asking my opinion, I've led far too many multiple lives to know what the truth is, or was, any more. And I can't say I miss it.'

'But if not for you, for other people. It is time for change, you have to acknowledge that.' She was looking at him earnestly.

'I would say good luck to you, truly. You may be ahead of the times, I'm sure you are. But you do have a large mountain to climb. If I'm not the one to help you there will be others who can. Perhaps you could write to Seigneur Stanislavsky and ask if he could spare a few roubles from his vast family fortune.'

Oddly enough that same thought had occurred to Merry and she had dismissed it. Anything connected to

Stanislavsky himself would inevitably have to involve Nicholai, which rendered it out of the question.

'Or Granville Barker. Have you tried to look him up since you've been back?'

'No.'

She felt suddenly deflated. It was a ridiculous idea, far too high a mountain, as Bertie had put it. She had neither the resources nor the will, not right now.

'Don't be downhearted, dear heart.' Bertie took her hand and squeezed it. 'It's wonderful to have plans, and dreams, the bigger the better. So I'm told.'

He let go of her hand. 'The problem with the *avant garde*,' he lowered his voice, 'is that while it is utterly noble, and I'm sure necessary, it does require access to considerable funds in order for it to be able to thumb its nose at audience reaction and commerce completely. Even I might contemplate dabbling in it if someone had the wherewithal to pay me. And pay me properly.' He laughed.

I hate Bertie, thought Merry.

'So when I say in my view you are not truly cut out for the *avant garde*,' he gently pinched her cheek, 'take it as a compliment.'

'I don't know how to take it.' She swiped at his fingers as if they were an annoying fly. 'I don't know what you mean.'

'You are too embedded in your family background,' Bertie continued complacently. 'The daughter of a military man and all that. Even if you are estranged.'

He was becoming more infuriating by the minute. Merry sat back in her seat and silently huffed.

'But I tell you what, Merry,' he began with new energy, as if the thought had only just occurred to him. 'I've an idea for you. The Actress' Franchise League. It's right up your street.'

She shook her head.

'Why are you wagging your head at me? You don't even know what it is, I'll be bound.'

'I've heard of it. I can guess what it is.'

Her melancholy had settled on her like a shroud and she was determined to keep it there.

'They'd love to know all about your Stanislavsky thing, they'll be up for a talk about it at the very least. Would you like me to arrange it for you?'

'Oh Bertie, stop interfering!' She almost spat it out. 'Anyway what have you got to do with the Actress' Franchise League?'

'In an honorary capacity of course. They are not too mean-spirited to exclude the support of the darker sex, even the ones who secretly wear skirts. Especially the ones who secretly wear skirts.'

He waved at somebody across the room.

'Don't let me detain you,' said Merry.

'Don't be ridiculous. I came here to be with you. I sense you are in the doldrums, it's not hard to detect. I sense these last few months have not been easy for you.'

Again, and without looking at her, he took her hand, and this time she did not draw back.

'I sense somebody broke your heart. Maybe the Russian fellow, whatsisname.'

She did not respond, and still he did not look at her.

'Every actor must have a broken heart at some point. Every person. It changes one's perspective. That's if you allow it to.'

Yet another person telling her misery was good for a person. It was enough to make a person spit. She drank her wine and said nothing.

27: The Academy

It was as the new term began that Meredith decided quite suddenly to take her teaching post at the Academy for Young Ladies in Gloucester Road a little more seriously.

Of all the things Bertie had said that had annoyed and hurt her equally was the notion that the daughter of a brigadier remains the daughter of a brigadier. In other words that it was all but impossible for a person, a woman in particular, to break from her past and create herself in her own image.

She had taken on her teaching position with a certain degree of cynicism, needless to say. What the Stanislavsky system could have to do with coaching young ladies to become socially-acceptable grownups – wives and mothers-who-never-put-a-step-out-of-line – she could not begin to fathom. And while she had made half-hearted and partly frivolous attempts to introduce The Master into the business of Deportment, Elocution and Manners, if only to make her own task more interesting, she had never truly put her mind to how His thoughts and His views could be truly incorporated into the lives of these young women. Women whose futures, as the daughters of the well-to-do, were mapped out for them in every detail. Surely there must be some among them who like her were just slightly tempted to break out of the mould created for them?

These spectacular thoughts became concrete, as spectacular thoughts tend to do, in the early hours of a sleepless night in Lambeth not long after her meeting with Bertie at the Salisbury. Everybody, from Bertie to Meredith to Gaye to a peasant farmer in Mongolia, is an accident of birth. In Edwardian England privilege was considered to be, well, privilege. A responsibility, a burden, a product of luck, not all of it good. A working class woman, despite her lack of privilege and opportunity but with fewer standards to maintain, had a freedom her better-off sister did not. Look at Gaye.

The point was, Merry's frantic brain went on, it is far too easy to dismiss the sort of young ladies who end up in Academies for Young Ladies as mindless, line-toeing younger versions of their mothers. It was a form of prejudice, if you thought about it. Why should they too not be given the opportunity to break out, to do anything they wanted to?

She was not advocating rebellion, that would be self-defeating, and doomed to fail, and inevitably end in her own sacking. Every rebel is an authoritarian, when you came to think about it. Every *avant-gardiste*, with his scorn for the popular and insistence on his own creative superiority has to be a bit of a dictator. 'My method is better than yours. If you do not follow my method you are a fool or a traitor.'

Her brain was definitely over-heating. But under the bluster there was the kernel of something that for lack of another definition she might call The Truth.

'The one thing I can do for these young women,' she told herself, 'is encourage them to find their own true selves.'

It was one of the noblest thoughts she had ever had.

~

At her next class she told the girls about an experiment she and her friend had once conducted on the streets of Manchester, when they had spent a morning 'in character', wandering in and out of shops and cafés as Dr Astrov and Sonya. The purpose of it was 'to get inside the characters' of Chekov's two fictional people, she explained, to see how they would react in ordinary everyday circumstances. It was an exercise Stanislavsky himself had invented, where he dressed as a tramp and went out and about mixing with other tramps. The idea was to see the world as other people see it. To be, for a short while, someone else, or as close as possible. As an actress she had found it both fun and remarkably illuminating.

So now she was going to ask them to do the same. To think of a character who was as unlike themselves as they could imagine and then go out and 'be' that character for the rest of the afternoon and report back. If you want to, she said, you can use the clothes from the costume department – yes, the Academy had everything. It is a serious exercise, she reminded them. They were not to be play-actors, and certainly not to show off. 'So, off you go,' she said.

The results were fascinating. Most of them chose to be working-class girls, with outlandishly implausible Cockney accents. The more convincing of them were surprised at how rude people had been to them, ignoring them or worse, passing lewd remarks. One or two of them found that part of it fun, and responded, with enthusiasm. One of them even admitted she found it 'liberating. You know, to be able to say what you think,' she giggled. Inevitably one pair took the exercise a step too far and pretended to be drunk, and on a whim of inspiration to have just attended the funeral of their father, so adding grief to uncontrollable behaviour. 'We just wanted to see what we could get away with,' they explained.

Whether or not the true purpose of the exercise had been achieved was a moot point. But when at the following class Merry suggested the experiment again, this time in a slightly different form, they were more than happy to comply.

'This time I want you to imagine,' she said to them slowly, and precisely, 'the sort of person you would like to be. In the future. This could be a rich woman living in a beautiful house in the country, with lawns and lakes and dogs. Or a happily married mother who spends her time frolicking in the park with her children, and dogs. Or maybe you are someone who is pursuing a career, or decided to study. To be a writer perhaps, or a teacher or even an actress.

'Once you have a clear idea in your head about this person I want you to become her, and to step outside once again and go about your business as her. Think about it carefully please, and seriously.'

The outcome this time was only moderately revealing. Disappointingly, the majority of the girls imagined themselves largely as older versions of themselves; well set-up in comfortable houses with servants – not too many – and pretty children and very handsome husbands. Merry questioned them on their choices. 'Is that who you really want to be when you're older?' she found herself saying, smothering the instinct to add 'Is that as far as your imagination can stretch?'

Be careful, she had to tell herself. You are here to observe, not to direct.

But among the rest was a quiet young woman called Camilla, who claimed the exercise had opened her eyes to a world she had never before witnessed. Her character, whom she had named Nora as her own name sounded rather frivolous, she acknowledged with a shy smile, was studying medicine in order to become a doctor. She had found herself in conversation – which she had initiated, she added bashfully – with a middle-aged gentleman in a restaurant. He was definitely a gentleman, she added quickly, and seemed genuinely interested to hear all about what she was doing – where she was studying, and what, and how demanding it was, and so on and so on; and most tellingly, she told them, what it was like "for a woman studying to do a man's job".

Here she paused. Meredith nodded. 'And what did you say to that?'

'I didn't know what to say,' Camilla acknowledged. 'I'd researched everything beforehand, you know, so I knew which institution I was attending, and how long was the course, and why I was so keen to become a doctor in the first place.' Here she paused, and gave her body an embarrassed little squeeze. 'I was thinking of Dr Garret Anderson. She was the first woman doctor, you know.' This she addressed to the room in general.

'In the end I asked him, politely, what he meant by the question. He was quite taken aback. I suppose . . .' she smiled, 'I had taken him by surprise by turning the tables on him, so to speak. He mumbled something about only men being suitable doctors, which rather got my goat. So I said that half the population were women and that only women doctors could fully understand a woman's body.' She flushed. 'I got the impression,' she resumed, 'he'd never really thought about it before. Whereas I had. Many times. He had just assumed that all doctors should be male. Just as all politicians, and lawyers, and so on. It made me realise that men make assumptions, based on the assumptions of their parents and their parents, and never question them. And why should they?'

She stopped finally. 'And is all this true, Camilla?' Merry asked. 'Are you hoping to become a doctor?'

There was a long pause as Camilla wrinkled her nose and turned to stare out of the window. 'Well I was thinking about it, vaguely. But then I thought probably it wasn't for me. It would be too demanding – not the work so much, as the – what's the word? – antagonism. I didn't think I was up to that.'

Meredith nodded. 'And now?'

'I don't know,' she shrugged self-consciously. 'I know I should, really. But, I don't know.' She tailed off.

Meredith opened her mouth to say something and checked herself.

She looked at the other women in the room. A few of them were staring at Camilla with a sort of wonderment. Others were gazing out of the window, or into the middle distance.

'What do you make of Camilla's story?' she asked them.

There was a silence. Then, 'She should be a doctor if she wants to be,' piped up one of them. There was a mumble of half-hearted agreement to this.

'It's easier said than done,' said another.

'I think she was very brave,' said one.

'Yes,' Meredith agreed. 'She was. Is.' It was the nearest she dared get to a comment.

As reactions went, it was disappointing.

Ah well, she thought. One step at a time.

It was not much more than a week later that she was summoned to the office of the Principal of the Academy, a neat, grey-haired, formidably aristocratic – in bearing if not in actuality – woman by the name of Miss Patience

Dell-Hathy. It was a meeting she had been half expecting. She had only met the woman once before, in the interview for the position which she now held. That she had been taken on in the first place, Meredith surmised, had more to do with her own background and bearing than anything else.

'Good morning,' said the lady. 'Do sit down.'

Her office was surprisingly small and austere. There was a rather plain desk, behind which Miss Dell-Hathy sat, upright, alert, smiling. A picture on the wall of some unknown aristocrat – an ex PM probably – and a wall of books and that was about it.

'I have received,' said Miss Dell-Hathy, in the last week, no fewer than three letters from parents claiming their girls had decided to . . . Now where is it?' She fumbled among her papers for a moment and brought out a letter. 'To become an actress.' She placed the letter down on the desk again and looked at Merry enquiringly.

'Really?' said Merry, trying to keep the delight from her voice.

'And another, here, from someone wanting to be a . . .'

'A doctor?'

'No. Now where does it . . .' She scanned the letter. 'Ah, here. An engineer.'

'Oh. Well, how splendid.'

'And the third – yes, here it is – a solicitor's clerk.'

'Well, that's interesting I suppose.' Camilla, whatever happened to you? thought Merry.

'It's all rather – coincidental, don't you think? Three letters expressing similar thoughts, all arriving within days of each other. Can you throw light on this?'

'I certainly can, Miss Dell-Hathy.' She proceeded to describe the experiments of the previous week, and in particular the second, when she had invited the girls to imagine their future exactly as they wanted it to be. She was about to go on to talk about Camilla and her ambitions to become a doctor, which she rather feared the girl was too frightened to pursue, when Miss D-H interrupted to say,

'Miss Martin, the purpose of this Academy is to prepare the girls for their future lives, in whatever society they find themselves and according to the wishes of their parents, who are paying for them. It is not our responsibility to encourage them to take up a career. There are plenty of other institutions that are far better able to do that, that are set up to do exactly that. That is not to say we are turning out groups of empty-headed young women who do not care about serious matters. As you know we have a debating society within the Academy, and we have classes in Current Affairs.'

How I would love be a fly on the wall of one of those, thought Merry.

'But it seems that here you have, forgive me for saying this, stepped out of line somewhat. It is not your fault, it is admirable that you have encouraged the girls to be so – creative. And as a woman with a career myself I have every sympathy. But here, today, is neither the time nor the place. Am I making myself understandable?' She smiled again, with some concern this time.

'Miss . . .' in her agitation Merry found she had forgotten the woman's name, but she ploughed on nonetheless. 'My concern is for . . .' she stopped, and began again. She told the lady about her own background, how her passion to become an actress had so antagonised her father she had been disinherited and was now estranged from her family. And while it grieved her, more than she could possibly express, the issue at stake was not just her passion for the theatre but rather her insistence on her own independence. That what she feared, for these young women, was that their desire for a career, or for a life that was in any way unlike the one they were brought up in, would be suppressed, to the detriment of everyone concerned.

'It seems so unnecessary,' she said. 'There is so much misunderstanding among families these days, not just because the daughter – it's usually the daughter – wants to break out and do what she really wants to do. Life moves on, you must know that yourself. Things are changing. Women are . . .'

'Do you lay no store by duty?' asked Miss D-H. 'And respect for one's elders?'

'Of course I do. But it works both ways. This is not A Midsummer Night's Dream.'

The Principal was momentarily nonplussed.

'These young women have their whole lives laid out for them,' Merry continued, in a rush. 'Not according to their own wishes necessarily – although in some cases maybe, in many cases probably, they are perfectly content. But for those who like to think for themselves, their options are pretty limited, don't you agree?'

'I understand all of that,' Miss D-H announced, calmly. 'Some women may want to break out of the family mould, so to speak. But not ours. Our girls are sent here on the understanding that they will be content to follow their parents' wishes. They are comfortably off, they can afford not to worry on that account. Many young women do not have the privilege of financial security behind them of course, and naturally, for them it is a very different matter.'

She could have argued back, indefinitely. But Miss Dell-Hathy's very calmness, her sense of her own rightness, was impenetrable.

Still, who would have guessed she had three quiet little rebels in her class? As she made her way down the corridor away from Miss Dell-Hathy's modest seat of authority Merry's smile grew wider and wider.

28: The bombshell

When she first heard the news from her friend Susanna Virginia suffered what she had heard described, but never before experienced, as a 'cold sweat'.

Ever since her visit to Lambeth the previous autumn and the discovery that Meredith was now living in Russia, after an initial period of numbness Virginia had managed to put all thought of her daughter out of her mind. While some might see that as callous or unfeeling, for the likes of the Mrs Stephensons of this world predictability was an essential. Why rock a boat that is steady and heading in a safe direction?

That is why ever since the rally the previous summer she had resisted her friend Antonia's repeated attempts to recruit her into the women's suffrage movement by inviting her to meetings or marches, as if she could wear her down through sheer persistence. Always Virginia came up with a feeble excuse that would fool no one, least of all Antonia.

The truth was Virginia's whole life was there, with her husband, within the walls of St Leonard's Terrace. It was where she belonged. True, there may be a bigger and more exciting world outside but for now all she wanted was peace and quiet. It was noticeable that since her brief excursion into the world of female rebellion there had been a distinctive cooling of the atmosphere at home. Being the people they were there was nothing said but everything implied. Conversation between Brigadier and Mrs Stephenson had become desultory, almost perfunctory. Virginia forced herself to avoid any topic that might be regarded as contentious, such as women's suffrage or, God forbid, the estrangement and subsequent exile – to *Russia* of all places – of their only child. By her own admission Virginia was not one of the world's natural rebels, and whatever feelings and instincts she might have once toyed with on the topic of women's independence and the right to vote, she was more than capable of sublimating them if necessary.

So when her friend Susanna announced she had heard from the daughter of a friend of a friend that a woman by the name of Miss Meredith Martin was now teaching at an Academy for Young Women in Gloucester Road her first reaction, following the cold sweat, was blind panic. While most mothers would rejoice at the news the daughter they thought had exiled herself to Russia was in fact not only living in the country but working a stone's throw from St Leonard's Terrace, all Virginia wanted was to think it was all a silly rumour, a case of mistaken identity.

But Susanna was adamant. She was even able to produce some horribly authentic-sounding detail, such as the time Miss Martin had invited her girls to go out and walk the streets 'in character', as her source has put it, an idea that originated from some theatre bigwig in Russia. The girls *adored* her, Susanna insisted. She was a breath of fresh air, and she had such interesting and almost *radical* expectations of them, why she even encouraged them to defy their parents if they felt their natural instincts were being suppressed because – and here came the bombshell – that is exactly what she herself had done.

Why was Virginia not overjoyed to hear all this? Granted, the fact that Meredith was working so very close to her family home, a few stops on the Underground, and had yet made no attempt to get in touch with her family was not something to be celebrated. And yet.

Should she turn up at the Academy, as she had done at Lambeth, unannounced? She was not sure she had the courage. Should she write to her daughter care of the Academy? That might be the best approach. And if she received no reply, what then? Could she face yet another rebuff?

Or might it just be best to do nothing and hope, just perhaps, that one of these days Meredith would get in touch of her own accord? That way the boat would stay on course. Yes, in the end that would definitely be best.

But she'd reckoned without Susanna. It was barely a week later that she arrived uninvited at Virginia's door with a pale young woman with unflattering hair in tow whom she introduced as her goddaughter Miranda, an introduction that induced such giggles in the girl Virginia assumed she was nothing of the sort.

She was, she explained, a pupil at the Roehampton Academy for Young Ladies. Why she thought she was being introduced to a middle-aged stranger named Mrs Stephenson did not seem to concern her.

'Well, do come in,' said Virginia. 'The house is empty, Maurice is out.'

She felt decidedly flustered. She was not good at being taken by surprise.

She ushered them into the back room. 'Do sit down. I'm sorry I can't offer you tea, it's Martha's day off.'

It was a lie, but she did not want to prolong this interview needlessly.

'Thank you Virginia.' Susanna took a seat near the

window and gazed out of it for a moment as the others settled one on either side of her.

'I told Miranda you were very interested to hear about the Academy,' she said, turning to each of them with a winning smile. 'And in particular about the lessons with Miss Martin.'

'Did you?' said Virginia. She did not intend to make this easy.

'So as we were passing,' she shot a look at her young companion, 'I thought why not let's drop in on Mrs Stephenson, and you can ask her anything you like.'

Then, when Virginia did not respond: 'Anything at all, can't she Miranda?'

'Of course, anything you like,' said the girl, who was sitting awkwardly on her hands and grinning.

'Such as,' said Susanna, seeing her friend was not obliging her, 'what exactly does Miss Martin do in these lessons?'

'Well, she is supposed to teach us Deportment and Manners and so forth, but actually,' Miranda giggled, 'she has us doing acting and so forth.'

'What kind of acting?'

'Well not the usual kind. She has us walking around pretending to be someone else. Once she asked us to pretend to be a person who was as unlike as we are in every way, so we . . .' more giggling, 'well some of us, we pretended to be cockneys, and prostitutes, and that kind of thing.'

There was a pause. Virginia said nothing.

'And then another time she told us to think of the person we'd really like to be in life, and go out and about and be that person. And that was really hard.'

'In what way?'

'Well.' Here Miranda paused for thought, and swung

her legs back and forth like a child. 'I'd never really thought about that kind of thing, you know, I'd always thought, I'd always assumed I'd be, you know . . .'

'You'd be?'

'Who I am now. Only older. And married, with children maybe. I never imagined I'd have to find a *profession*. I mean I don't mind earning my living for a while, you know, in something temporary.'

'Such as what?'

'Well, a lady's companion maybe, that's about all I'm fit for!' She laughed properly this time, before lapsing into silence again and gazing at the floor.

Virginia felt suddenly sorry for the girl. But she was not going to join in Susanna's game no matter how much she would have liked to quiz her.

'This term we're going to do a play,' Miranda volunteered after a moment. 'A Midsummer Night's Dream. I think that's what she said.'

Susanna glared at Virginia but Virginia's eyes were fixed expressionlessly on Miranda.

'So, what is she like, this Miss Martin?' asked Susanna.

'She's – well, she's a little strange to tell you the truth.' Miranda looked nervously from one lady to the other. Poor thing, how had she found herself in a situation like this? 'Strange but nicely so, if you see what I mean. She's an actress herself, and I think she wants us to be – well, not actresses, but somebody. She's very – unconventional. We like her very much.'

She smiled broadly and swung her legs enthusiastically.

'But we also think, some of us, we also think she may not stay long.'

'Why do you say that?'

'We think she may be in trouble with Miss Dell-Hathy.

Just . . . it's just a thought. She was summonsed to see her the other day and, well . . .' She shrugged and tucked her legs under her. 'All the best people don't stay long, they're not really cut out for it. It's a shame.'

'Who is Miss Dell-Hathy?'

'She's the Principal. She founded the Academy, it's her baby you could say. And what she says goes. Absolutely. That's why we have such a turnover of teachers, nobody who's remotely interesting or unconventional can stand it.'

'This play that you're supposed to be performing, can anyone come and see it?' Susanna asked.

'If you're family or a friend, yes, of course.' She was looking enquiringly at the two ladies. 'Why, did you want to come? I'm sure I could arrange that.'

'Not really,' said Virginia.

'We certainly would,' said Susanna, at more or less the same time, and continued, 'When is it to be?'

'At the end of the term, the beginning of July. I can let you know, and I will do my best to find you tickets. Is it just the two of you?'

~

'Who did she think I was?' Virginia demanded.

It was the following day and she was standing on Susanna's doorstep, out of breath and quietly seething.

'She thought you were a friend of mine who was thinking of sending her own daughter to the Academy,' said Susanna. 'As a pupil.'

'I'm hardly of an age to have a school-age daughter.'

'She's not to know that,' said Susanna blithely. She smiled. 'So now we have an opening, so to speak. We can use Miranda in any way we like. Won't you come in?'

'Thank you, no. What do you mean "use"? Poor girl, hasn't she been through enough?'

'She doesn't mind in the least. She said as much. She

adores Meredith – Miss Martin – she's only too happy to talk about her. Anything to keep her there I believe.'

It was a double-edged compliment, you could say. Virginia felt strangely proud.

'Do come in Ginger, it doesn't suit you standing on the doorstep haranguing me.'

'I said thank you but no.' And she turned and went.

But some sort of die had been cast, she admitted. It's difficult to opt out of life completely when you have a friend like Susanna.

29: The green, white and gold fair

'All actresses are suffragettes.'

Who said that? Maybe nobody, but it was certainly an assumption. An assumption that an independent woman who earned her own living automatically supported the campaign for women's suffrage. If there was anything that annoyed Meredith more than anything it was an assumption, and yet while she was prepared to go some way to avoid being part of the herd on this occasion she also had to acknowledge that it had been such a long time since she had trod the boards she barely felt she could call herself an actress.

So when a writer acquaintance contacted Merry and invited her to appear in a short play she had written to be performed at a 'fair' at Caxton Hall organised by the Women's Freedom League, whoever they were, while in normal circumstances she would hardly have jumped at the chance to appear in some propagandist snippet for no pay, there were on this occasion other considerations: not least the fact that the event was to be attended by Everyone in the Acting Business and in particular Ellen Terry herself and her daughter Edith Craig. Which is why she found herself accepting.

It was not that Merry was anti women's suffrage. It was an issue that did not concern her unduly. If asked she would have struggled to tell you which party was in Government, let alone who the Prime Minister was. In this she considered she was not unlike many of her contemporaries, whose lives were unlikely to be affected by whether or not they were able to vote.

Nonetheless there she was arriving at Caxton Hall just before noon on a day in April.

It was like stepping into the pages of a children's book of fairy tales. Every inch of surface was adorned in green, white and gold, as befitted the title of the three-day event. The hall was festooned in banners: greeting new arrivals was the declaration "Dare to be free", and "Stone walls do not a prison make". Smaller banners dangling from the ceiling depicted suffragette 'martyrs' who had served prison sentences for the cause, and countries that had already embraced female suffrage and survived, each of them framed in laurel wreathes and gold stars. Around the edges of the hall was arranged a series of stalls selling all manner of home-made artefacts from needlepoint to ceramics. In one corner there was a replica of a prison cell, in another an entertainment booth advertised artists of the likes of Marie Lloyd, and a small stage promised drama from Ellen Terry and, of course, Meredith Martin.

It was all thoroughly theatrical and quite overwhelming. Even Merry had to pause to catch her breath.

At noon on the dot the great lady herself appeared, costumed bizarrely in a long green robe embroidered with gold, a heavy bead necklace and a headdress resembling a Valkyrie, with huge padded earpieces. All of which, Merry learned from a stallholder who was dressed likewise, was a representation of a time back in the fifteenth century when women apparently enjoyed a higher status and greater freedom than they did today in the twentieth.

A small child appeared with a bouquet which she shyly presented to Miss Terry, at which point the great lady sank to her knees and smothered the poor thing in kisses. She then gave a heartfelt and highly theatrical speech expressing her pleasure at being chosen to open this splendid bazaar and wishing the organisers great success in the raising of funds for the women's cause.

Meredith's play was a witty yet silly little piece featuring a tug-of-war between the mother and governess of a sixteen-year-old girl for her soul. The young girl was played by a sweet young thing called Felicity – 'You may call me Filly' – whose sole concern was for her appearance and who resisted anything she was made to do that required the slightest seriousness, such as thinking and learning. 'Frowning is *so* bad for the skin,' she complains. The mother meanwhile is happy to indulge her daughter, indeed to take very little notice of her, so when she is not present the governess, played by Meredith, gets to work on her charge by attempting to induct her into the suffragette movement. On discovering what the governess is up to the mother becomes apoplectic; but thanks to her supreme patience and eloquence the governess manages not just to talk the daughter around but the mother as well.

It was a slight piece but fun to play, and the reaction from the (necessarily biased) audience was far more enthusiastic than it merited.

Afterwards Merry stayed on to watch the next presentation. It was a short play without words featuring an altercation between a six foot policeman and a suffragette a foot smaller, during which the little woman caused her antagonist to lose his balance, his helmet and his dignity through her skill in the art of jiu-jitsu. The audience, and Merry along with them, roared their approval as the little suffragette acknowledged her victory while standing on the back of her prone adversary.

This was followed by a demonstration by the lady suffragette, who turned out to be a teacher of the art – or science, as she called it – of jiu-jitsu. It involved, she explained, three branches: the simple self defence designed to resist a violent attack, which entailed the use of arms and elbows and a constant alertness; the throw, which required a good deal of practice; and finally the throw followed by the rendering of the assailant unconscious by means of neck locks. The first, the lady explained, was designed to protect a woman from being physically manhandled and injured by a Person in Authority, in particular the Police, or an abusive husband. The second and third were only to be used in instances of extreme threat, from a burglar or a lunatic. Knowledge of the art should, she explained, be in every woman's repertoire if she could ever expect any kind of equality with men.

It was a sobering thought, if not immediately appealing to Merry.

Later in the afternoon she attended a performance of a one-act play called *How the Vote Was Won*, by Cicely Hamilton and Christopher St John. ('Christopher St John' was the pen name of woman called Christabel Marshall, a close friend of Ellen Terry's daughter Edith Craig.) The play was set on the day of a General Strike for women called by the suffragettes to test the government's assertion that women did not need to work as they were supported by their menfolk. Into the living room of hapless anti-suffragist Horace Cole and his wife Ethel marches a stream of female relatives from his sister to his niece, an aunt and a number of distant cousins, all demanding to be taken care of according to the edicts of the government. Finally and at the end of his tether Mr Cole marches off to Parliament to demand votes for women.

Once again the play was received warmly and with hilarity from what was obviously a partisan audience. Which made Merry ponder on the purpose of the whole enterprise. She passed the intervals between entertainments browsing the wares on sale in the stalls and occasionally entering into desultory conversation with actress acquaintances. Teaching Deportment and Manners to over-privileged young women in an obscure Academy in Gloucester Road is not necessarily something one boasts about, especially to one's peers and contemporaries who were – she did not need to hear this – progressing so much farther in their careers than Meredith.

It was a diverting day one way or another. The atmosphere was cosy and complacent as persists among groups of people who agree on absolutely everything. How it might have advanced the cause of women's suffrage, or freedom – apart from raising money – was moot.

On her way out Merry was accosted by a middle-aged woman with a mass of black curly hair, who introduced herself, surprisingly, as Countess Mollie Russell.

'Would you like your tea leaves read, my dear?'

It was clearly a rhetorical question.

'Sit yourself down here. There, now all I do is boil the kettle, make the cuppa.' She spoke rapidly, without pause, and in an Irish accent. 'And all you have to do is sit there and say nothing.'

Which, despite Merry's natural inclination and out of sheer curiosity, she did.

The lady then proceeded to regale her recruit with the details of her colourful life, how she was born in Country

Galway the daughter of a shoemaker, the aristocratic connection was by marriage – her third – to Earl Russell. She was a passionate member of the Women's Freedom League . . .

'And who, exactly, are they?' Merry enquired politely.

The Countess paused, annoyed at the interruption. Then she laughed and said, 'We're the Women's Freedom League dear girl, don't you know who we are?' And carried on, outlining for the clarification of her meek listener her programme for the rest of the month, giving a speech here, attending a rally there, meetings, meetings, lobbying Parliament, it was clear the Movement was for the Countess all-absorbing. And the tea leaf reading?

She did not seem inclined to expand on that. Instead, as she prepared the tea she asked, 'Are you a sceptic, darling? Don't be afraid to admit it, many people are. It's just useful to know.'

Merry was tempted to tell the Countess about the cards, about how they had led more astray than she would have believed possible. That she was not a sceptic, rather worse, she was a disappointed believer, perhaps an agnostic but not yet quite an atheist.

'No, I'm not a sceptic,' was what she said.

'Good.' As she poured tea into a white china cup the lady said: 'Think of a question.'

'What sort of question?'

'Anything you need an answer to. Think of it as you drink. Don't tell me. There.' She placed the cup and saucer before Meredith. 'Hold the cup firmly, it needs to feel your energy.' She sat back and folded her arms. 'Think of your question as you drink,' she repeated.

Of course, Meredith's mind was a complete blank. The most obvious question – 'Will I ever be a leading light on London's stage?' – seemed in the circumstances too obvious, and general, and besides she wasn't sure she wanted to know the answer. 'What does the future hold?' was even more vague. She ended up sipping the tea, which was black, and bitter, and thinking of nothing whatsoever.

'There, now, leave a little liquid at the bottom of the cup,' the Countess peered into Meredith's cup and nodded in approval. 'Grand. Now, take the cup in your left hand and swirl the leaves thrice from left to right.'

Merry did so.

'Now very carefully and still with your left hand, turn the cup upside-down on the saucer and turn it slowly three times. That's it. Pause a little.' She closed her eyes and sat stock still for a whole minute before she opened them again and said, 'Now turn the cup back upright and place the handle to the south, to the Fourth House, which is here.' She pointed to her left and Meredith obeyed dutifully.

There followed a long moment while both ladies gazed into the cup.

'What do you see?'

Meredith hesitated. She saw a pathetic cluster of sodden leaves scattered randomly around the base and sides of the cup.

'I see a random mess of tea leaves,' she said half-heartedly.

'Dearie me, no no,' said the Countess. Without moving the cup she indicated with a long fingernail. 'Here, close to the handle, this is your domestic life. Here,' the fingernail moved to the opposite side, 'is the world outside', to the rim, 'this is the present', to the sides, 'the future' and finally to the base, 'the future again, the distant future.'

'So?'

'Something Significant here.' The fingernail moved to

the side of the cup near the handle. 'Are you married? No? So. You soon will be.'

'Absolutely not.'

'Ah, they all say that. But you can't argue with the tea leaves. As for your career – you are an actress, I take it? Of course you are, why else would you be here? Hmm. Well, there is not much to see here.'

Merry leaned back in her seat and scowled.

'No need to look like that. Keep an open mind, that's what I always say. Don't just turn your back on the prospect of domestic harmony. Not,' she added quickly, 'that I can claim to be an expert on that.'

She laughed again, and pushed back her hair.

'Keep an open mind, darling,' she repeated. She leaned across the table at Merry and gazed deeply into her eyes. 'You just never know what's around the corner.'

With which she stood up, picked up the cup and saucer and turned her back by way of dismissal.

That was it, thought Meredith as she made her way to the exit. All soothsayers are charlatans and liars, they only want to forecast marriage and domestic bliss, I made that mistake once and never again. She was a fully-fledged atheist now.

Besides, in that minute while waiting for the tea leaves to settle, or for inspiration to strike Countess Russell, she had had an Idea.

30: Secret acts of defiance

'Girls, can you keep a secret?' asked Merry.

They were gathered around her so tightly they were all but sitting on her lap. Gazing down at their eager faces she realised they would do pretty well anything she asked of them, bless them. She had grown surprisingly fond of them all, even of mousy little Miranda, with her nervous giggle and her simply dreadful hair. What some mothers imposed upon their daughters was tantamount to child cruelty.

She had not told them of her interview with Miss Dell-Hathy, though she had no doubt they had an inkling, nor about the letters. And while she was bursting with curiosity to know who the three rebels were, and in particular the would-be actress, she had the common sense not to ask outright.

'We're going to do a play,' she said.

'A Midsummer Night's Dream?' piped up one of them.

'No, we're not going to do the Dream. We're going to do a play called How the Vote Was Won. But we're going to *pretend*, to the outside world, that we're doing The Dream.'

Sometimes she found herself talking to them as if they were children. They were not stupid, she had not to forget that, they knew precisely what she was up to.

'Is that a suffragette play, Miss?' This came from a pert little thing called Rosamund.

'It certainly is,' said Meredith.

There was a buzz of excitement.

'It's about women's dependency on men. Apparent dependency. One of the reasons the Government doesn't think it right to give women the vote is because they believe all women are dependent on their nearest male relative – their husband or their father, or even their brother. So the women declare a one day general strike, they down tools and head to the home of their nearest male relative and place themselves at his mercy. What do you think of that?'

'Poor man,' said a girl called Amanda. The others giggled.

'Poor man, indeed. And in this case, that man, called Horace, happens to be an ardent anti-suffragist. But when he sees all these women pouring through his front door – his sisters, his cousins, an aunt or two, some of whom he's never even met – he panics, understandably.'

'And off he goes to Parliament to declare his support for the suffragettes!' cried Rosamund. Merry had no doubt that Rosamund was one of the rebels.

'Why does it have to be a secret?' asked a tall, serious girl called June.

'Why do you think?'

'Because Miss Dell-Hathy does not believe in women's suffrage,' said Amanda.

'How do you know that?'

It was an assumption, Amanda asserted, otherwise she would have let it be known, and quite probably she'd have gathered them all together and marched them down to Parliament to break a few windows.

'Are there any suffragettes in the room?' Merry asked.

Not one hand went up.

'You know this is a safe place,' she went on. 'I keep your secrets, you keep mine.'

'My mama says the suffragettes are misguided,' said a ginger-haired, pouty, pretty girl named Guinevere. 'She says no one ever got anywhere by breaking the law. Besides, she says she is already mistress of the house and my papa does everything she tells him to so she has no need of the vote.'

They laughed at this, all but Guinevere herself.

'Have any of you discussed women's suffrage with your parents, or with anybody??'

One tentative hand hovered.

'Yes Evangelina?' What ridiculous names they had, thought Merry.

'Well, Miss. I think my mother would like to be a suffragist. Not a suffragette. My mother believes in the vote, she said as much. But she doesn't believe in breaking the law either.'

'Not all suffragettes break the law. Suffragists are law-abiding, and they've been campaigning for years,' said Rosamund. She went on to explain, without prompting, precisely and confidently, the background to the women's suffrage movement, founded initially and peacefully by Mrs Millicent Fawcett – the sister of Dr Elizabeth Garrett Anderson – and more recently they were joined by Emmeline Pankhurst and her daughters. (Thank goodness someone here knows so much more than I do, thought Merry.) The peaceful ones were called suffragists and Mrs Pankhurst and her lot were suffragettes. And *that* was where it was all going wrong, Rosamund went on without drawing breath, as their aim was to be as disruptive as possible, which is why they were so unpopular among so many people.

'And what else are they supposed to do if they've been ignored all this time?' Amanda demanded.

And on it went. In no time at all there developed a fierce, overlapping and largely pointless argument between the militant-sympathisers and the others, if they could be so-called, while Merry sat back and watched, not without considerable satisfaction. It didn't take much to wake them all up. So they did have a view on the matter even if they weren't quite sure about following through. Not all the girls joined in, but that did not mean they were not engaged. Which among them might be the rebel letter-writers? Rosamund most likely, and Amanda, but who else? Not June. Certainly not Miranda, or Guinevere. Quite likely a dark horse like Ruth, who barely spoke but always listened intently, or maybe . . .

'Girls!' She was afraid their noisy eagerness might rouse the interest of the Principal. 'A healthy argument is a wonderful thing, but please just keep your voices down!'

They quietened, as if by magic, and sat back down on the ground land looked up at her in silence.

'So that is how we will spend the term,' said Merry finally. 'We will spring a surprise on everyone right at the end.' She gave them a beatific smile.

'And now you may go. And remember, not a word to anyone.' She placed a finger on her lips and most of the girls did likewise. How young they were, she thought. How horribly, ridiculously young.

She was aware as the room emptied of one girl who remained where she was, sitting on the floor, fingering a strand of hair that had escaped from the tight bun its fellows had been forced into.

'Miranda! Miranda? Come here.'

She did so. She stood silently before Merry, still fiddling with her hair, swaying from foot to foot.

'Who does your hair, Miranda?' she asked her gently.

'My hair? My mother. Why?'

'Does she ask you how you like it done?'

'No.'

'What about your clothes?' She knew the answer to this already. Miranda appeared to have only two outfits, one a musty blue with faded lace at the cuff, the other a faded grey with no lace at the cuff.

'Mama chooses everything,' she said shyly. 'I'm only sixteen, I don't know my own mind yet.'

It wasn't surprising.

'Who says? Your mama?

Miranda nodded. She looked quite crestfallen.

Merry nodded. 'Would you like me to show you a new style?' Then when Miranda did not immediately reply, 'Because forgive me for saying it, but I don't think it flatters you. Not at all.'

Miranda's face fell, and for a horrible moment Merry thought she was about to cry.

'Here. Turn around.'

She did so, and Merry gently unpinned her hair. 'I believe it's important to develop one's own style, don't you agree? After all you may only be sixteen but in a short while you'll be leaving the Academy and then you'll be let loose on the outside world – I don't have a hairbrush, you don't happen to have one with you, do you? No? Ah well, we can do what we can. And if there is anything a woman needs to learn it's how to look her absolute best.'

The pins were out now, dozens of them, they sat heavy in Meredith's hand and she wondered how the poor girl managed to keep her head upright under all that weight.

Miranda's hair was, not to put too fine a word on it, lank. Someone – the mother presumably, or the maid under instruction from the mother – had coated it in some sticky substance, seemingly to keep it in place. It could do with a good wash and a sound rinse.

'Next time you wash your hair, rinse it in vinegar and lemon juice,' she told the girl. Miranda nodded mutely.

She ran her fingers through Miranda's hair. It was thick, and given half a chance and a reprieve from the fearful products some women insisted on applying to their hair in order to give it structure, it could be quite lustrous. Merry could have been quite jealous of it. As it was, her fingers were becoming stickier and stickier and she was beginning to feel quite sick.

'You should wear your hair loose, Miranda, it suits you. It makes you look much softer.' All this was true, but there wasn't much anyone could do with it right at that moment.

Miranda closed her eyes as she stood before her teacher and relaxed under the gentle touch of her fingers. It was clearly not something she'd ever experienced before.

'We were talking about you the other day, to a lady,' she said after a while, still with her eyes closed. 'She was asking about you.'

'Who was?'

'She's a friend of my – godmother. Sort of godmother. Mrs Gulliver.'

'Susanna Gulliver?'

Miranda nodded.

'What was she like, this friend?'

'She was, she had dark hair, with silver bits in it, drawn back from her face, with a clip. Like this.' Miranda mimed a hairclip on the top of her head.

'Did she have a pair of spectacles around her neck on a chain? A silver chain?'

'Yes, I believe she did.'

'And did she wear an emerald ring on her left hand? '

'I don't know. I didn't notice.'

'Was her name Mrs Stephenson by any chance?'

Miranda looked at her impassively. 'She didn't introduce us. We just called on her unexpectedly . . .'

'At St Leonard's Terrace?'

'Yes! How did you know?'

'Just a guess.' Meredith drew a deep breath. 'What did she say, this Mrs Stephenson?'

'She said very little. It was Mrs Gulliver who asked all the questions.'

Merry nodded. 'All right, Miranda,' she said dismissively. 'I'm sorry I can't do much about your hair at the moment. Would you like me to pin it up for you again?'

'No thank you, Miss Martin.' She tossed her head like a pony, and giggled.

'What will you tell your mama?'

'I'll say I had to let my hair down for the play. For Hermia.'

'For Hermia?'

'Yes.' She looked at Merry wide-eyed. 'Because we're practising for A Midsummer Night's Dream, aren't we?'

Merry laughed. 'God bless you, Miranda. Here, don't forget these.' She held out the pins.

'Thank you Miss Martin.' She took the pins and pocketed them, and with a delighted wave she ran – skipped – across the room and out the door.

So. Her mother was on her trail. Or by the sounds of it, she was being coerced onto it. Merry knew Susanna Gulliver well enough, she was a trouble-maker, a busybody. It would not surprise her to know it was Susanna Gulliver who was behind her mother's secret arrangement with Mrs Vlatsky. Yes, it was beginning to make sense.

Well, it was not her problem. Now her mother knew where she was it was up to her to make contact, if she dared. She had more important things to think about.

She was excited about what lay ahead. Now the writing was on the wall at the Academy, even if she had written it herself, she intended to go with a bang rather than a simper. At the same time she did not want to frighten the girls merely for her own gratification. It was not their fault they were born into privilege. It was not their fault they had been sent to this ridiculous academy, whose only real purpose was to ensure they stayed within the boundaries set for them with as much elegance as they could muster and a lovely speaking voice, but also with no encouragement to think. It was not education. It was a form of indoctrination.

And while new Merry, new kinder, more thoughtful Merry knew enough to acknowledge not everyone is or wants to be a rebel, if she could encourage her charges to begin to think for themselves, as Miranda had just demonstrated with her tiny act of defiance, then her job was done.

31: Freddy

She felt rather than heard the footsteps following her down the street. She quickened her pace and they did too. It was tiresome, this silly game of cat and mouse, even in a respectable district like Gloucester Road. In many ways she felt safer among the slums of Lambeth, where nobody had anything to steal so nobody tried to rob you in the street.

She stopped dead and he all but crashed into her.

'Ah,' he said.

She whipped round. 'Freddy!' It was surprising bearing in mind how long it was since she'd seen him how quickly his name came to her. 'What are you doing here?'

'I was following you.' He was panting. 'You keep up quite some pace. I was waiting for you by the door, you walked right past me.'

'How did you know where I worked?'

'There are ways and means. How are you, Miss Makepiece with an 'i'?'

She stared at him for a moment. She felt unexpectedly wrong-footed.

'I am very well, thank you. How are you?'

And without waiting for an answer she continued on her way.

'Meredith, wait a moment!' He grabbed hold of her

sleeve and she pulled away from him as if she was about to robbed. 'Is that all you can say after all this time? Did you get my letter?'

Merry's hand went automatically to her handbag. 'I did, yes.'

'And did you not feel fit to reply?'

Embarrassment was not a familiar feeling for Merry, but right now that is exactly what she felt.

'I'm sorry,' she replied nervously. 'I didn't know what to say.'

She stared at the ground.

'What happened to the Russian?' he asked gently. And when she did not reply he said: 'Come, let's find a café. Please.'

He took hold of her arm, gently this time, and she allowed herself to be led past the Underground station to a neat little place in a side street away from the main road. He chatted as they walked, aimlessly, about this and that, their surroundings mostly, which he seemed to know. Then as they were seated and he had ordered tea and scones he lent across the table and said 'I am very pleased to see you again after all this time. I meant every word of it. What I said in the letter.'

'I'm sorry,' Merry said again. She was not meeting his eye. 'I did intend to reply, I just didn't know what to say.'

'Dear girl.' He turned to look out of the window. 'You never cease to surprise me.'

'Did . . .' she hesitated. 'Did you mean what you said? Truly?'

'Of course not,' he said. 'I was playing games. Of course I meant what I said, why would I pretend about something like that? I can be serious when I try, you know.'

There was a slight pause as the waitress arrived with

the tea.

'Your performance, if I can call it that, that day at the Criterion, was nothing short of a revelation. You walked onto that stage as Meredith Martin, actress *extraordinaire*, and after an hour of battering and bullying that was frankly very painful to watch you became a human being in all your nakedness. Not just a human being but a truly, utterly riveting player. Actress, player, performer, none of those words do you justice. You were transformed, in front of all those critical eyes, into somebody so unlike yourself it was verging on the miraculous.'

He poured the tea.

'And now I have embarrassed you. Which is not easy to do. Do you take sugar?'

'No thank you.'

'I wanted to tell you so at the time but you were, shall we say, distracted by the maestro.'

'Yes, that is true.'

'All of which I told you in the letter. I was hoping for some kind of acknowledgment at least, maybe even a thank you.'

'I was busy. There was so much going on. And I left Lambeth for a while. I didn't get your letter till some time later and I . . .' She tailed off.

'You were hoping to go to Russia but it didn't quite work out like that. I'm sorry, I genuinely am.'

'You seem to know a lot about me.'

'I made a point of it.'

He was watching her steadily but her mind was, or appeared to be elsewhere.

'It was a – moment, in my life,' she said. 'I made mistakes, big mistakes, I was swept off my feet, to coin a cliché, and I should have known better.'

Freddy stirred his tea.

'And what I learned, that day at the Criterion, and in the months that followed, I thought I had been transformed, as an actress and maybe as a person. And when he left . . .' she paused for such a long time she almost lost the thread. 'I found myself with nothing. Not just no home and no hope, but all that work, how could I put it into practice? What has Stanislavsky to do with anything, unless you're playing Chekov? I thought I'd truly broken through, I'd broken down barriers, but in the end,' she shrugged, 'I'm back where I was before, older but no wiser.'

'I don't agree.'

'How would you know?' she snapped, and then relented. 'Sorry Freddy. You see I am no different to the stuck-up prig I was when we worked together.'

'I don't agree,' he said again. 'I saw you change, before my eyes. I don't believe you're the same haughty soul who stood on stage with me at the Court. I simply don't believe it.'

She stared at him, or rather, so it seemed to Freddy, through him.

'Won't you drink your tea before it's cold?'

She picked up her cup and looked into it.

'I had my tea leaves read the other day,' she said, with a smile. 'For what it was worth.'

'And?'

'Oh, I can't remember. Nothing of any importance.' She drank, thoughtfully.

'I'm not here to declare my love for you, if that's what you're concerned about.'

'It never occurred to me,' she lied.

'Whatever I may have said in my letter. Implied. But somehow I seem to have frightened you off.'

Merry placed her cup down carefully on its saucer and,

reaching into her bag she pulled out the letter.

'You carry it with you?' Freddy's eyebrows lifted. 'My, I'm flattered. Should I be flattered? What are you trying to tell me, if anything?'

'That I was embarrassed, yes, and surprised, certainly. And yes, I was deeply moved, if you really want to know. Which is why I didn't reply.'

'I see, I think.'

She was still holding the letter. 'I composed several replies in my head, some of them quite . . . But I really didn't know who I was then. I was transitioning you could say, from old Meredith to new Merry. I used to be called Merry you know.'

'It doesn't suit you.'

She laughed. 'Well it did once. And then I thought people will never take me seriously with a name like that. So I became Meredith.'

'People never take people seriously who take themselves seriously.'

'You're probably right. Anyway I tried being Merry, in name and in nature, but it didn't work.' She lifted her cup again and this time she drank from it. 'I'm a good teacher you know.'

'I'm sure you are.'

'I took on this position out of desperation really, I thought I could bluff my way through it somehow, at least until something better came along. But then I began to get rather fond of the girls, I felt a responsibility to them. I know what it's like to have one's future mapped out for one. It's not easy being born to the upper classes you know.'

Freddy laughed. 'I'll take your word for it.'

'So I tried an experiment, using some of the ideas Nicholai taught me. It had nothing to do with acting, more to do with stretching the imagination. I asked the girls to walk around the streets in the character of another person, someone as unlike themselves as possible. They enjoyed that I think. So then I asked them to do the same, this time as the person they would like to be in their future lives. I stirred them up.'

'You would.'

'Unfortunately the Principal didn't see it that way. I'm on borrowed time now. But I don't care. I have one parting shot up my sleeve, if I can say such a thing.'

'Which is?'

'I'm producing a suffragette play called How the Vote was Won.'

'So you're a suffragette after all?'

'I didn't say that. I'm producing it under the guise of pretending to do A Midsummer Night's Dream, just to get them thinking.'

'You're playing a dangerous game. I wouldn't expect anything less from you.'

She looked at him through narrowed eyes but he appeared to be serious.

'You say you're the same person you were, but that's far from the case. The old Meredith would never have taken this sort of a risk, not to say found herself teaching in the first place, and taking it so seriously.'

'That's true.'

'Nobody could go through what you went through in public, on stage in front of hundreds of people, and not be changed. Not to mention what you went through subsequently.'

He reached across the table and took her hand and she did not pull back. 'I like the new Meredith,' he said.

'Merry.'

'That Nicholai fellow, he was a weird one. But

whatever else he did to you, or didn't do, he transformed you as an actress. And I imagine as a person. If you could hang onto that, rather than – the other thing – all in all it might turn out to be one of the better episodes of your life.'

Merry withdraw her hand from his, slowly. 'You are at least the third person to tell me how wonderful it is to have your heart broken. I don't see it.'

'Would you rather it had never happened? That you'd never turned up at the Criterion that day?'

She thought long and hard about that.

'Not really,' she said.

'There are you then,' said Freddy.

32: Rehearsals

For the likes of Miranda Pettigrew future prospects in the first decade of the twentieth century did not look too promising. She was not pretty like Evangelina or even Guinevere, with her ginger curls and her winsome expression. She did not have the assuredness of Rosamund or the sharp intelligence of Amanda. What she did have was an overbearing mother who chose her clothes, her hairstyle and her opinions, and no doubt in time her entire future, the sum of which gave her the appearance of a child much younger than her sixteen years. At best she might expect to find a second-rate husband who married her for the family inheritance. Otherwise she was doomed to spend her life as a lady's companion, God forbid, or as an unpaid nanny and servant-of-all-work for her beastly brother.

On the other hand what Miranda did have was a Secret: a Secret that involved her teacher and her teacher's own Mother, from whom she was evidently estranged, for whatever reason, which in turn gave Miss Martin an added air of mystery and even exoticism.

When Miss Martin not only removed the ton of hairpins from Miranda's head but then ran her fingers through her hair – or tried to – the girl almost fainted with joy. It was a long time, perhaps the whole of her life, since anyone had touched her with something approaching tenderness. It was at that moment that she looked into the lovely, hazel, inscrutable eyes of Miss Martin and fell in love.

Whether or not Miss Martin was aware of this was unclear. There was a distance about her, almost a sternness, that was at odds with the gentle woman who toyed with her pupil's hair. Miranda began to wonder about her teacher's life. Unmarried – and she must have been in her mid-twenties at least – estranged from her mother and no doubt her father too, a failed actress who was forced to earn her own living teaching in a silly girls' institution like the Roehampton Academy. It must have been a big comedown for someone like Miss Martin, who, as she was wont to tell her charges not once but several times, had appeared on the West End stage twice, once under the management of Herbert Beerbohm Tree no less. (Miranda had heard of Beerbohm Tree, she wasn't quite sure where or in what context.) She imagined a tragic story of loss and abandonment, maybe at the hands of a married man, which was the reason for her family problems and for her professional downfall.

She felt sorry for Miss Martin. She also felt she had a special bond with her, she wanted to be her confidante.

Unfortunately Miss Martin did not seem to see things the same way. She cast Miranda in her suffragette play as a girl called Rosie, a character she had invented, Merry explained, to plump up the cast as she had more pupils than there were parts in her play. It was a non-speaking role but one, she claimed, that was crucial to the plot in some way she did not quite explain.

So Miranda felt snubbed, and let down. She rather wanted to cry but her pride forbade it.

The lead roles in the play were allocated, predictably,

to Amanda and Rosamund and, less predictably to Ruth. To those that have shall been given more. The central role of Horace, the humble, put-upon clerk, was played by June, the tallest girl in the class, and 'his' wife by Guinevere.

Rehearsals were enormous fun. Miss Martin encouraged the girls to play around with their characters, to experiment, to be as outrageous as they dared. She invited them to try out their characters in the outside world ('though not at home – remember our secret, ladies'). Some of the girls in Miranda's opinion were simply showing off. It was not how she imagined a play was put together, in her view Miss Martin was nothing like authoritative enough, allowing all that mayhem. She was not yet ready to acknowledge this approach gave the girls the freedom and permission to break away from their natural self-consciousness and restraint.

The play was, of course, in the nature of a farce. By pointing up what might happen if all women did as the Government instructed and gave up their employment to arrive at the doorstep of their nearest male relative and place themselves at his mercy, how could men be expected to cope with no one to cook for them, clean their offices or serve tea in teashops? It may be satirical, as Miss Martin explained, but behind the comedy lay an important message.

As for Miss Martin herself, she found she looked forward to these rehearsals with surprising enthusiasm. It was astonishing what these girls were capable of if they were allowed to let their hair down on occasion. More than one or two of them – Ruth for certain, and quite possibly a chirpy soul called Petra, who had perfect comic timing – had the makings of fine actresses, given the chance, and of course the will.

She was aware of Miranda's disgruntlement. There wasn't much she could do about it, except single her out from time to time for praise – praise which didn't convince anyone as there was very little anyone could do with a part that entailed hanging onto the sleeve of the elegant, forthright Mrs Christine, played with aplomb by Amanda – until she was shaken off, and sulking thereafter.

'Don't moan quite so audibly, Miranda,' she instructed her at one time. 'Your role is not to distract from what else is happening on stage.'

That was it.

Infatuation can so easily turn on itself. That night as she lay in bed a beautiful woman appeared to Miranda in the guise of Miss Martin but when she opened her mouth to smile she revealed rows of broken, discoloured teeth, and as she reached out to touch the girl's hair her nails became six inch claws and her hazel eyes began dripping blood, at which point Miranda opened her mouth to scream and woke up.

The following day in a break in rehearsals she said to her teacher, in a voice far louder than necessary since she was standing right next to her: 'Why does your mother not speak to you, Miss Martin?'

Merry turned to stare at Miranda for a long moment. 'Gracious me, where did that come from?' she asked.

Miranda pouted. The whole room had gone quiet and every head was turned in her direction.

'Isn't that true? She doesn't want to see you, or to speak to you.'

Merry regarded the girl coolly. My my, how the worm turns.

'It is true, as a matter of fact, Miranda. She threw me out of the house – or rather my father did, with my mother's agreement – because I wanted to become an actress.'

There was a pause. Merry turned to face the rest of the girls and smiled. 'It's what happens.'

'They threw you out of the house?' gasped Evangelina.

'As Miranda knew. I had thought it was our secret,' she looked to Miranda, who glared directly back at her. 'But I don't suppose it really matters. Maybe it's as well you know what some of us women have had to go through in order to do what we really want to do.'

'Is it anything to do with women's suffrage, Miss?' asked a girl called Nancy.

'Not directly, no. As you know I am not a suffragette, not as such. But it is all part of our demand for equality, you could say. I am not aware of any men who have been disinherited because they wanted to be actors.'

'Disinherited?' someone whispered.

'Although I suspect they may be one or two. It's an odd world we've been born into girls, but one that's changing fast. I have no doubt by the time you get to my age it will all seem very different. Or I hope it will. It's up to you, all of you, to make sure it is.'

'I want to be a suffragette when I'm older,' said Nancy.

'I too,' said Gertrude.

The quiet ones were speaking up now. 'I hope you won't need to be,' said Merry. 'I hope there will be no need for suffragettes when you're older. But no doubt there will be other issues you can turn your attention to. Equal pay. Equal status, within marriage especially. It's probably not something your parents have discussed with you and it's certainly not something you will learn at an Academy such as this one. But that doesn't mean you have to accept your lot without question. I hope you know that.'

Miranda started to cry. No one seemed inclined to comfort her.

'I loved my parents dearly,' Merry went on, with a glance in Miranda's direction. 'I still do. But I didn't agree with them. I didn't think they had the right to lay down the law with me.'

'You stuck to your guns,' said somebody.

'I did. And then pride stepped in, which is why we have stalemate. I am waiting for my mother to approach me, and I wouldn't be surprised if she's not waiting for me to approach her.' She shrugged. 'I don't regret what happened, not for a moment. You have a lifetime ahead of you so you'd better decide now how you want to spend it.'

There was silence. Miranda snivelled.

'Especially you, Miranda,' said Merry.

There was a bit of a pause as Miranda made a monumental effort to pull herself together.

'Did you ever want to get married, Miss?' asked Evangelina.

'Not particularly. I'm not against marriage, but – you know me well enough, I would not make an easy wife. I've had things my way for far too long.'

'But you're still very pretty, Miss,' said Nancy.

'Yes, you are,' said Petra.

'And well-turned-out,' said Guinevere.

Merry bowed her head graciously. 'Thank you girls.'

'And it's never too late,' said someone.

'She has her career,' said another. 'That's what's important to you, isn't it Miss Martin?'

'Why did you give up acting to teach here?' asked a small girl with dimples.

'I haven't given up acting, Daphne. I came to teach here because –' she paused for a second. 'Because the opportunity came along. And to be quite truthful I've enjoyed it more than I expected. Much more than I expected.'

'Then you're staying on, Miss?'

'I don't think so. I don't think . . .' Now that truth was in the air, what the hell? 'I don't imagine I will be welcome here for much longer. But it's been a pleasure, truly, and a privilege even. And I have learned something about myself. Always – if I can pass on another piece of wisdom, so-called – keep an open mind. Pleasure and satisfaction can be found in the strangest places.' They stared at Merry with different degrees of understanding, or lack of. Miranda gazed up at her through tear-filled eyes, which she wiped roughly with the back of her hand. Merry saved a special smile for her.

33: How the Vote Was Won

The hall was packed, but as Merry stepped out onto the tiny stage she deliberately directed her words to the back wall in order to avoid looking at the audience in case she spotted her mother among them.

'Ladies and gentlemen,' she said. 'I have a surprise for you. You were expecting a version of Shakespeare's A Midsummer Night's Dream but what you are about to see is very different. It's a modern play called How the Vote Was Won, written by two women. The reason for the change is partly practical, as in the short time available I didn't think we could do justice to Shakespeare's comedy, and partly because as I'm sure you will agree our play is of much greater relevance to today's young women and the life that lies ahead when they leave this Academy. We have had so much fun putting it together, I hope you have as much fun watching it. Thank you.' She bowed, and allowed her eyes to skim quickly over the sea of upturned faces, too quickly to make out any of them, including the Principal, whom she assumed was sitting in the front row.

There was a bit of a baffled silence, followed by some murmurings and a smatter of applause as Merry bowed again and exited.

It began tentatively. The audience, taken by surprise, were still getting over their bafflement. But as one by one the various relatives – sisters, cousins, aunts and nieces, some of them complete strangers – walked in through Horace's door, clutching suitcases and trunks of belongings, so the audience began to respond, and thus the cast grew in confidence and timing. When it came to the announcement that naval volunteers had been drafted in to act as charwomen at the House of Commons and non-commissioned officers were stepping in to take the place of striking waitresses at Lyons & Co, they laughed long and loudly. 'Wait for it,' Merry muttered in the wings, 'wait for the laughter to die before you carry on.' Which miraculously they did. The news that all the police forces in the country had been brought in to cope with the miles-long queues outside the workhouses – where women without relatives had been instructed to assemble – and that the PM was unavailable for comment because he was busy making his bed with the assistance of the boot-boy and a foreign office messenger brought more prolonged laughter and even the odd cheer. How extremely odd, thought Merry, coming from what she assumed to be predominantly the mothers of her young students. And how exceptionally pleasing.

There were six curtain calls. Even Miranda smiled. The excitement was total. Rosamund broke into a jig. Merry, watching from the wings, wiped away a tear.

'Dear ladies,' she said afterwards, in the dressing room. 'You excelled yourselves, every one of you. Congratulations, and thank you.'

'Thank *you*,' they said. And 'Did you see Miss Dell-Hathy's face?' They shrieked with laughter.

Merry went cold. 'Tell me.'

Daphne pulled down her mouth and scowled.

'She disapproved.'

'I think she did.'

'My mama was scowling all through,' said Guinevere sulkily.

'That's a shame Guinevere, but you can't win them all,' said Merry, ruffling the girl's hair. 'I would hope they enjoyed the play and the performances even if they didn't necessarily go along with its message.

'My mother loved it. She *loved* it,' said Rosamund. Merry had not seen this rather serious girl so lively before. 'My papa too, I think. It really woke them up.'

'How about you, Miranda?' asked Merry. 'Was your mother in the audience?'

Miranda nodded.

'And do you think she enjoyed it?'

Miranda shook her head. She was close to tears.

'Dear girl,' Merry took Miranda's hands in hers. 'Don't be upset. Some people's ideas don't change, no matter what you do. It's hardly your fault.' She gave Miranda a quick hug. 'The important thing, the important people, are you. All of you. What you think, what you truly believe. You've been subject to strong influences in your lives and there will be many more to come. You need to know your own minds and to follow your own instincts – not your parents', or your teachers', and certainly not mine. I hope you've learned something from me, and from your other teachers and especially from Miss Dell-Hathy, who is only following expectations.' She smiled at them. 'And she's not a bad sort, not really. But we don't know everything. None of us. You need to have the courage of your convictions, or even your lack of them, if that makes sense. And if I've done anything to encourage that, then I feel duly proud of myself.'

There was a long silence as Merry stood in the centre of the room and gazed at the young things about her.

'And now I think I may be about to cry. So if you don't mind, I'll just slip . . .'

And off she went, out of the room and down the corridor and out through the tradesmen's entrance into the street and away, far away from the Roehampton Academy for Young Women for the very last time.

34: The end is another beginning

That evening Merry sat down to write a letter to Miss Dell-Hathy, politely tendering her resignation and explaining that while she was fully aware of Miss D-H's disapproval and that she, Miss Martin, had overstepped the boundaries of what was expected of her in producing a play about women's suffrage, she had done it with the best of honest intentions. That it was her firm belief that in this rapidly changing world today's young woman needed to have more at her fingertips than an ability to run a household and produce children. That it would not be long before women were competing with men for the same employments, on the same terms, and if they were not properly prepared they risked being left behind. No matter what one's views may be on the question of women's suffrage surely it was not too much to suggest every woman should have the right to determine her own future, was it?

She thought long and hard over her words. Finally, as satisfied as she felt she could ever be, she signed the letter, placed it in an envelope, sealed it and stamped it and walked to the post box on the corner of the street. Then she returned to her room, undressed, lay down on her bed and drifted to sleep thinking about How the Vote Was Won.

It was though she said it herself a minor triumph. They had performed with an assurance beyond her wildest expectations, despite their over-protective backgrounds. She chuckled at the memory of June as the put-upon lowly clerk Horace Cole always one step behind, whose growing bewilderment she so eloquently expressed by means of an increasingly slack jaw. And Ruth, who rarely opened her mouth in class but somehow was able to produce a wonderfully affected drawl as Horace's exotic music hall comedienne cousin. Even Miranda got the odd laugh from her sulky expression (which was not a huge leap for Miranda, truth be told). The enthusiasm, the *commitment*, oh dear, how she would miss them.

Anybody could produce a play with clever actors. But this – working with well-mannered young women whose every spontaneous thought and action had been firmly stifled from birth – this was real accomplishment. Who'd have thought she, Meredith Martin, was capable of encouraging these girls to surprise themselves so profoundly?

She dreamed that Freddy came to call. Hands in his pockets, big grin on his face. 'Up you get you layabout – what sort of time is this to be still in bed?'

'Freddy, what earthly business is it of yours when I choose to be in bed?'

'It's not. But you have an important visitor.'

'Yourself, you mean.'

'That too. And another.'

Of course it wasn't a dream. It was noon, daylight, and Freddy was standing right there in her bedroom, laughing down at her.

She tried not to show her embarrassment.

'Give me a moment, I'll be right down.'

He sauntered out of the room, hands still in pockets.

An important visitor. No, it couldn't be. And yet knowing Freddy it probably was. Knowing Freddy he had somehow tracked down her mother and even invited her here to Lambeth. How dare he?

She dressed quickly, splashed cold water on her face and ran a quick comb through her hair.

He was downstairs in the front room chatting away to Mrs Vlatsky as if they were old friends. Mrs V's eyes were flashing, her face lit up as Merry arrived. 'Here she is, at last. I am telling your friend how tired you must be, you are not usually in bed at this time. He does not believe me! He does not believe anything I say!' Her hands flew to her cheeks and she laughed merrily. 'But now I will leave you two together.'

She made to leave the room and turned back. 'And if there is anything you need . . . I have offered tea, or . . .'

'No thank you Mrs Vlatsky, you are very kind.'

And she finally went.

Merry walked slowly to the fireplace. She had a strong sense of foreboding. Freddy watched her closely.

'You do look tired,' he said.

'It was quite a day.' She stood with her back to him for some time.

Then: 'Look Freddy, if you've done what I think you've done, I do not appreciate it. There are some things in life that are not your business, believe it or not.'

Freddy rocked on his heels. 'I do indeed believe it. Can I ask what you're referring to in particular?'

Merry glared at him. 'The important visitor. There's only one person it could possibly be.'

'Who? The King? The Prime Minister?'

'Don't be silly. You know who I mean.'

Freddy scratched his head. 'Shall I explain?'

'I think you'd better.'

He stood still for a moment, thinking.

'To begin at the beginning,' he said. 'I was there yesterday, watching your play.'

'Yes, I thought you might be. How did you come upon an invitation?'

'I – er – know some people.'

Merry nodded, and waited.

'It was absolutely splendid. Such a good afternoon, the audience enjoyed it very much, with one or two exceptions of course. You have some very talented students.'

'I had.'

'Had. Ah.' He thought some more. 'Yes, I see. Anyway, I got talking to this woman, she . . .'

'She what?'

'Give us a chance, dear girl. She was one of the parents, mother of the girl who played – Mrs Christine, I think it was. Amanda? Amanda.'

'Yes. So?'

'She was asking about you. When I told her we were old chums, that we'd worked together and so on, she wanted to know all about you. Your background, your history and all that. So I told her.'

'And?'

'Well, she obviously thinks very highly of you. Evidently Amanda has been talking about you and the sort of things you've been doing in class and, well, in a nutshell she wants to help. Amanda's mother, that is.'

Merry blinked. 'Help in what way?'

'Financially. She realises you are leaving the Academy and she wants to help you set up on your own in some fashion.'

He paused.

'They are obviously pretty well-heeled.'

'Set up on my own? As what?'

'As the Principal of your own establishment.'

'What sort of establishment?'

'That's up to you. Or so I gather. That's why she is on her way now, to discuss possibilities.'

Merry gazed at Freddy blankly. She shook her head. 'What makes you think I want to do such a thing?'

'It's nothing to do with me. I'm just the messenger. Also, I had the feeling she might not be alone, that there might be other parents who'd consider chipping in.'

'"Chipping in"?' Merry harrumphed. 'You make me sound like a down-and-out.'

'I wouldn't put it quite like that. But it's an opportunity, take it or leave it.'

Merry began to pace the room. 'I don't know that I'm ready for this,' she muttered, mostly to herself. 'I'm not very good at thinking on my feet, it's all too . . .' she tailed off. 'And in any case,' she stopped to face him, 'how is it that you seem to get involved in the oddest things, Freddy? Had you met this woman before?'

'Of course not!' Freddy took his hands out of his pockets for the first time. 'Don't keep thinking this is all some great conspiracy, it was not my idea, I just happened to get chatting to the woman and, well, here I am!'

'Here you are.'

She gazed at him long and hard. She really couldn't fathom Freddy. For all his easy-going manner and his apparent insouciance he was full of surprises.

'What do you stand to gain from all this?'

He looked at her in astonishment. He scratched his head, like a parody of a music hall comedian.

'Dearest Merry, stop looking for ulterior motives when there are none! None at all!' He threw his hands in the air melodramatically. 'I am being as transparent as a – sheet of glass. I stand to gain the prospect of your good fortune and happiness, which will bring me joy enough. Does that answer your question?'

For all his frivolity Freddy had never even tried to flirt with her. Perhaps he was not of that persuasion. Despite her cool manner Merry was used to men flirting with her as a matter of course, actors in particular, even married ones – married ones especially – it was part of the game. She felt almost insulted. Freddy's stand-offishness – if it could be called that – was in itself a puzzle.

'You can turn her away if you want, there is no obligation, and no hard feelings. She should be here very shortly. Would you like me to stay or shall I make a quick get-away?'

'I feel distinctly cornered.'

'I'm sorry about that, it wasn't intentional. She was very insistent. Perhaps it's best if I leave you to talk to her alone.' He wrinkled his forehead in concern.

She didn't reply to this. She didn't feel able to make any kind of decisions about anything.

'Yes,' said Freddy finally. 'I think that might be best. I'll call back later to see how you got on. Or maybe tomorrow,' he touched his forelock, 'if I may be permitted. May I?'

Merry nodded numbly.

35: Merry's quandary

Freddy did not come to call the following day. She stayed in all day waiting for him, and when he did not arrive, nor the day after, Merry began to panic. She realised she had no way of contacting him, she had no idea where he lived, or worked, if he was working. How was she supposed to make a decision without him?

Four days later he was there, offering apologies but no explanations.

'Where have you been?' She almost pulled him physically through the front door.

'I do have a life, you know. I'm sorry, I was busy.'

She took him to the front room. Mrs Vlatsky, to her relief, was absent.

'It's been four days! Had you forgotten?'

'I never forget things. Calm down dear Merry.' He took a seat and crossed his legs. 'Nice weather for the time of year, don't you think? Not too stiflingly hot. I do detest London in the summer sometimes. One longs for open spaces. And water. Lakes and things. The sea even. Are you all right? You look agitated.'

'Well that's hardly surprising. Not a word from you and I had no idea how to get hold of you.'

'I am always get-holdable, eventually, you should know that.' He swung his free leg. 'So tell me all.'

And so she did. She told him of the elegant, tiny lady, dressed from head to toe in mint green, who had arrived as expected and greeted Merry on the doorstep in great excitement as if she were royalty. How she refused to sit down throughout the interview and began by describing, at huge length, the effect the performance of How the Vote Was Won had had on her. How it had opened her eyes not just to her own daughter's abilities but to the whole business of women's suffrage which, she confessed, she had dismissed as an idle and unnecessary distraction from what she had always regarded as a woman's place and duty in life, which was to serve the family. That it had taken her several minutes to recognise her own daughter, who was playing a woman twice her age and from a background that could not be more different than her own. How she had felt awake for perhaps the first time in her life, she would never look at the world, or her daughter, in the same way again.

None of this seemed to surprise Freddy. 'Go on,' he said.

It was not just the play that had affected Mrs Amanda, as Merry called her. She had noticed subtle changes in her daughter's behaviour – 'Nothing untoward, you understand,' she said hurriedly – so she had begun to quiz her on her days' events at the Academy and had heard about Merry's experiments sending the girls out onto the streets imagining themselves to be other than who they were. That when Amanda first announced to the family that she was thinking of pursuing a profession in the law her mother's first response had been surprise and shock – 'horror even, or at the least total bewilderment'. But then they had sat down, mother and daughter, and 'had a good long chat about all sorts of things,' including Merry's experiment, which had set Amanda off on her path in the first place. 'And I realised, for the first time, how *conventional* and traditional we had been with her. It had honestly never occurred to me before that Amanda's prospects should be in any way different to my own. Never occurred to me. I knew she had a brain, more than her mother, or her father too, come to it, but that need not be a problem if properly handled. She always seemed comparatively compliant, so I never questioned – *we* never questioned – or even thought very much about her upbringing. It just happened.'

It was at that moment that, apparently exhausted, Mrs Amanda finally sank into an armchair. She took out a handkerchief and dabbed at her eyes.

'But seeing her there, playing a woman so unlike herself, and so apparently *comfortable*, well, it set off all sorts of thoughts in my mind. Not very coherent ones, for the most part. I was seeing – someone quite apart, not my daughter, nobody I had ever met before. And yet, so *believable.*'

She paused. Merry, who had been standing stock still, patiently waiting for her visitor to get to the point, sat down opposite her and said nothing.

'And I realised – and this will sound foolish maybe – that Amanda is not the person I had thought, had assumed, she was. She was a modern woman. And she – they – all of them, this world is not the world we were brought up in. It was a . . .' she stopped, and looked into space.

'So will you allow Amanda to follow her ambitions to become a lawyer?'

'What? Oh that, yes. Well, we need to discuss . . . That is not the point. It's not what I came here for.'

'Ah.'

'You.' She looked up suddenly. Her look was quite

fierce. 'I don't know who you are or very much about you at all. But you have what I can only call a quite remarkable gift.'

It sounded almost like an accusation.

'Well, thank you.'

'I don't know how to describe it. I've always thought of actresses as rather – don't misunderstand this please – as not the most intelligent people, you know. Pretty of course, with lovely frocks and hats and so on. I never thought actresses really had brains, and imaginations.'

Merry nodded and tried not to laugh.

'So in a nutshell, I – we – would like to offer you the means for you to open up your own Academy, to do whatever you would like to do in whatever way you would like to do it.'

Merry did not respond.

'I know this comes as a shock – to me as well as you by the way – and I haven't really thought it through. But I wanted to tell you, before I've had a chance to come to my senses, and to talk it through with Mr Egerton, my husband – I have my own money, you see. And I think, I rather believe, that there are one or two other mothers who are thinking along similar lines. So together, we could do it together, we could think about it.' She paused, tucked her handkerchief back into her handbag and looked at Merry and frowned. 'What do you say?'

'And what did you say?' asked Freddy.

'I said I'd think about it. That there was a lot to think about, and I'd never – well, actually it's not true, I had, once, thought about, with Nicholai, you know, briefly – but the idea of running my own Academy had never really been on my score card. That there was a lot to take in, and what sort of establishment she had in mind, and she said that was entirely up to me, I would have free rein to do

just what I've always done, only more so.' She stopped
and looked at Freddy apprehensively. 'It's a bit far-
fetched, isn't it?'

'Not at all,' said Freddy.

'I've never run anything before, I wouldn't know how
to.'

'You could get someone to run it for you.'

'And besides, I'm an actress.'

'Indeed you are.'

'I like to act.'

'It needn't stop you.'

'Oh but it would, of course it would. So, what do you
think?'

'I think it's a crazy idea.'

'Yes, it is, I agree.'

'It's all too easy,' said Freddy, 'for an actor to run away
with a sense of his own importance. But we're puppets
really. We bring other people's words to life, that's no
mean feat, but we're no more than channels for other
people's ideas. The really powerful ones are the writers,
and the teachers.'

'So?'

'I'm just thinking aloud. An actor is never in charge of
his own destiny, unless you're an Irving perhaps, or a
Tree. It's a terrible life for the rest of us.'

'Why do you keep doing it then?'

'Laziness, mostly. And curiosity. To see what crops up
next. But to have real influence – not all of us want that,
mind – that's another matter.'

'What are you really saying?'

'No more than I am actually saying. I wouldn't dream
of trying to persuade you either way, you'd never forgive
me.'

'I can't . . .' she hesitated. 'I can't do this on my own

Freddy.'

He looked at her sharply. 'Gracious. Of course not. Nobody is expecting you to do anything on your own.'

She leant across to him and reached out a hand, and he took it and held onto it, and eventually he said: 'I'm with you, whatever you decide.'

'Are you Fred?'

'You know I am. I've been with you – perhaps that should read 'you've been with me' – ever since that day at the Criterion.'

'Oh.'

'I would like to suggest we could embark on this adventure together, but I fear you would run swiftly in the opposite direction.'

'What do you mean?' she dropped his hand.

He took a deep breath.

'Well now, how should one put this?' He uncrossed his legs and crossed them again the other way round. 'Meredith Martin, Miss Proud-as-Punch as you once were. Miss Keep-off even. Your message was very clear. Until that day at the Criterion. And what happened – subsequently.'

'You mean . . .'

'Him, the Russian. I admit that took me by surprise. That you of all people would firstly allow yourself to submit to his bullying tactics, in full public view, and would then be swept off your feet by such a person to the extent that you pledged yourself to him in *toto*, as I understand it.'

'How did you know about that?'

'I made it my business. So I began to rethink. You, acting, the whole box of tricks. You weren't the person I thought you were.'

Merry nodded and allowed herself to smile. 'I was not

the person I thought I was.'

'Life's a funny thing. And when I heard you hadn't fled to Russia in the first place, that it had all gone rather horribly wrong . . . dear me.' He paused.

'What?'

'I wanted to come running, to fold you in my arms and comfort you, to stroke you, to do all sorts of utterly ridiculous things. Thank God common sense intervened.'

'I don't understand what you're saying, Freddy. You never even flirted with me.'

He looked at her in surprise. 'Of course not, I wouldn't have the nerve! You were not the sort of person a fellow flirted with. And I knew – well, you only had to look at him, what was his name? The way to this woman's heart was through some perverse form of mortification. Come now, you have to agree with me.'

She opened her mouth to speak but said nothing.

'It's terribly hard for a man sometimes, you have no idea. I don't have many natural bullying tendencies, it's not my nature, so what's a man to do? Pretend to be other than he is? Stay aloof and distant when all he really wants to do . . . *Really* wants to do is be as soppy as a puppy.'

'You? A puppy?'

'And now I've said far more than I should have. I've ruined everything.' He got to his feet and stretched. 'I will be on my way.'

He made for the door and she did not stop him.

36: No man is an island

If one wasn't careful one's life could be taken over by total strangers. First it was Mrs Amanda, who had taken it upon herself to organise Merry's future without any participation from her. And then not a few days later it was Miranda, turning up unexpectedly on her doorstep, who in her naïve and quite unintentional way was about to add trauma to turmoil.

It was not a comfortable feeling for the likes of Meredith Martin, mistress of her own destiny, answerable to nobody. Now there were people who appeared to be waiting for her decisions on *their* ideas for *her* future. Who did they think they were?

And Freddy. Vanished again before she had a chance to ask him what he'd meant that day. Was he propositioning her? Surely not. *Freddy?* Fred was not the propositioning type, she couldn't imagine him contemplating anything so serious. Not Fred.

Life could get so terribly muddled at times.

And then Miranda, of all people. How did these creatures find out where she lived? It's as if Mrs Vlatsky had posted a notice on the outside of her house – MEREDITH MARTIN LIVES HERE. Heavens above.

She had arrived very early in the morning, around 10, before Merry was completely up and ready. She stood on the doorstep physically shivering with fear, almost incoherent.

'I'm sorry to come here like this, I hope you don't mind, I won't keep you long, I just wanted . . .'

'Come in Miranda, come in.'

She led the way down the hallway to the front room. Whatever the girl wanted Merry did not particularly want their conversation to be overheard.

'So, what can I do for you?'

She looked as if she was about to cry. 'You went without saying goodbye.'

'I thought I'd said goodbye to you all. I didn't want to prolong it, if that's what you mean.'

'They say you're leaving.'

'It's more a case of being gently pushed, you could say.'

'And that you're thinking of starting another academy, of your own.'

'Well, now, where did you hear that?'

They were both standing. Merry put her hands on her hips and, when the girl took an involuntary step backwards she said. 'Oh, sit down, please. And tell me why you're here.'

And Miranda had done so, in her faltering manner. She had heard on the grapevine – it was being talked about, the girls, someone had mentioned it, she forgot who. And the point was, she wanted to know, if it really was the case . . .

'Yes?'

She would like to attend. To attend Miss Martin's new academy, as one of her founding pupils, or even as her assistant. She was sure – no, she had not discussed it with her mother, not exactly, but she felt she could persuade her. And she felt so sorry, *so* sorry, for what she did in rehearsals.

Meredith looked at her blankly.

'What did you do in rehearsals?'

'When I told them your secret. About your . . .' she swallowed.

'Oh, good gracious. That. I had forgotten. It's all water under the bridge Miranda, I don't suppose anyone took much notice.'

'But the point is, she was there.'

'Who was?' She was beginning to feel one step behind, an odd feeling for Meredith.

'Your – mama. At the show. I saw her. And she spoke to me afterwards, she was with – my godmother.'

'Your god – oh, you mean the lady who took you to see my mother? Susanna Gulliver? Well, she would, wouldn't she?'

'And she asked me to give you a message.'

'Which is?'

'She said . . .' Miranda swallowed again. 'She said to tell you she loved you very much. And she thought the play was – terrific, that was the word. No, it wasn't. Tremendous.'

'Tremendous.'

'I think that was it. She wanted me to tell you that.' There was a pause. Miranda fidgeted. 'She was crying.'

'Was that it? The message?'

Miranda nodded, and bit her lip. 'I think so. But then Mrs Gulliver said you should come and visit.'

'Mrs Gulliver? Why should I want to visit her?'

'No. Visit your mama. That's what Mrs Gulliver said.'

'And did my mother have anything to say about that?'

'She didn't . . . she didn't contradict her.'

They sat there for a moment in individual contemplation.

'That's all, really.' Miranda began to edge awkwardly out of her chair.

'Thank you Miranda.'

'That's all right.' She hovered. 'So, if you do start an academy – will you tell us?'

'I have absolutely no idea. About anything.'

And that was it. Miranda had stood there for who knows how long, waiting for she knew not what, for a sign, or a dismissal. And when Miss Martin continued to stare fiercely into space Miranda tiptoed to the door and out of the house.

How *dare* they? These – strangers, or near strangers. How dare they interfere in her life so? She felt her entire existence was under threat. New directions, new decisions, and now her mother. Her mother, whose non-presence loomed so enormous in her consciousness she almost blocked out the light.

Something had to be done.

~

'What's up, my dear?'

It was Mrs Vlatsky, tapping quietly on her bedroom door. It was not a thing she customarily did, although Mrs V was very conscious of her lodger's moods, more so than one might give her credit for.

'I haven't seen you for days. Are you eating?'

'More or less.'

'You look very pale.'

She was not dressed. Eleven in the morning and she looked as if she had not slept a wink.

'I have a lot on my mind.'

'Would you like to tell me?'

Who, Mrs Vlatsky? Of course not, how could she begin to understand the world Meredith moved in?

But then this was a new world, a world in which the

likes of Mrs V took Meredith by the hand, literally, led her downstairs and into the front room where she sat her down and went off to make tea, and Merry did not try to object.

And over tea she told her, everything. The Academy, the play, Freddy, and now the girl Miranda and her mother. All of it happening at once. And Merry, caught in the middle of it, trapped like a wild animal while the world whirled around her at dizzying speed and she was helpless to stop it.

'So what is exactly the problem?'

'I just told you.'

Mrs Vlatsky raised her eyebrows slightly. 'I see no problems. You have opportunities. People want to help you. How is that a problem?'

'I like to make my own decisions, thank you very much,' she snapped.

'No man is an island,' said Mrs V.

Merry looked up at her. 'What?'

'"No man is an island entire of itself; every man

Is a piece of the continent, a part of the main."'

'John Donne. What does he have to do with anything?'

'You, my dear. You think you can exist entirely on your own, with no help from others. Why? Nobody can do this.'

'There's a difference between help and interference.'

'It depends how you see it. You have friends who offer you help, you refuse them. Every time. This way you will stay alone for a long time.'

'Explain yourself, Mrs Vlatsky.'

'Your mother, this woman, Freddy, all of them love you, you want to push them all away. Go away! Leave me alone!' She threw her hands in the air melodramatically and even Merry could not suppress a smile. 'Why? What is this – independence?'

'What do you mean they all love me?'

'Your mother loves you very much. I know this. And Freddy too.'

'How do you know?'

'How do I know Freddy loves you? Because he told me so. "This wretched woman, I do love her you know, Mrs Vlatsky". He says to me these words. "But you are not to say anything. If she has the slightest hint she will run away in the opposite direction."'

'Did he say that?'

'He said that, exactly.'

'It does sound rather like Freddy,' Merry acknowledged.

'And then you waste your time on the Russian, who did not love you.'

'That's not true!'

Mrs V looked at her under her eyebrows. 'Mairie,' she said, as if to a small child. 'Now you listen to me.' She sat forward in her chair and placed her hands squarely on her knees. 'One of these days, who knows, you will be a mother.'

'I doubt that very much.'

'Stop!' Mrs V raised an admonishing finger and Merry jumped in surprise. 'Do not say that. "I don't want, I don't think" – always no no. <u>You do not know.</u>' She emphasised each word with a slap on her knee. '<u>You – do – not – know,</u>' she repeated. 'Do not refuse what you do not know. And when, and if you become a mother, you will know true love, perhaps for the first time. And you will understand things in a way you do not now understand. And you will take – ' she gestured accordingly, 'grab what you can when you can. Because love is precious. Love is the most precious thing.'

'You are not telling me anything I do not already know,

Mrs Vlatsky.'

'I am not *trying* to tell you things you do not know!' She was almost crying with exasperation. 'It is not what you do not know, it is what you do not choose to see!' She leaned back in her chair, as if exhausted, then immediately leaned forwards again. 'You must allow people to love you, and to love them back. Allow the thought. Do not block. Always you are blocking. "No, I do not believe in love, I am not interested to fall in love, I am interested only in my work. My <u>work.</u>"' She pumped her knee again. 'Yes, I understand this. And you think you can do all this alone. "No lovers, I do not need lovers, I do not need a mother. I do not need friends. I am alone, and all-powerful, and I will do things <u>alone.</u>" So.' She paused and glared at Meredith. 'Open the door.' She gestured again. 'Just a little. Let them in.'

She sat back in her chair again and continued to stare at Meredith.

'I rather think it's up to them to come to me, if they really want to.'

Mrs V raised her arms into the air and let them fall again. 'That is exactly what they have been doing! What else have they been doing, all of them, but coming to you, one after one, offering this and offering that . . .'

'Besides,' Merry interrupted, 'I don't know how to get in touch with Freddy, he didn't leave me an address.'

'He wrote letters to you?'

'He did, yes, you know that.'

'His address is on the letters?'

'I don't . . . well maybe, I don't suppose I looked.'

Mrs Vlatsky nodded. 'Your mother, you know where she lives.'

'Of course I do.'

'Well then.'

And then, as if she'd suddenly remembered an urgent task, Mrs Vlatsky got to her feet and left the room without a further glance at her lodger.

37: Decision time

After that things went quiet. Horribly quiet. Nobody called. Nobody wrote. Mrs Vlatsky went about her daily business as usual although she kept a certain distance between herself and her lodger. When Merry asked one morning, tentatively, if she might want to read her cards again the good lady shook her head with some vehemence and said, 'You do not need the cards to tell you what to do.' Which was shocking, in its way.

You do not need the cards to tell you what to do.

Maybe she was not the independent soul she had imagined herself to be. Why else would she have fallen for the cards' prediction in the first place? Had she fallen in love with Nicholai because the cards had told her to? No, that was ridiculous.

The following morning she was up before nine o'clock for the first time since she left the Academy. She spent longer than usual over her dress, and her hair, and by half past ten she had left the house and was making her uncertain way on foot across the brand new Vauxhall Bridge to Pimlico.

He opened the door before she even had time to ring the bell.

'At last!' said Freddy.

Now she was there she did not quite know what to say.

'You've made a decision? Wait here a moment.' He disappeared and reappeared moments later with a jacket. 'It's not as balmy as one might expect in August. Come.'

He took hold of her arm and steered her away from the house and down the street towards the river. 'Very fresh,' he pronounced, sniffing the air like a dog. 'I can feel autumn in the air. I love autumn, the gradual turning of the leaves, the mist and mellow fruitfulness – or is that spring? – no matter, it's a gentle time of year and the sun is kinder, when she appears that is.'

He squinted up into the cloudy sky. 'How have you been? You are looking better than when I saw you last, you have colour in your cheeks. Dearest Meredith.'

There was a fresh easterly breeze. He found them a bench facing the river and offered her his jacket.

'No thank you Freddy,' she said.

They sat together for a minute looking out over the river in silence.

'Is it my turn to speak or yours?' Freddy asked.

'The river looks very different from here,' said Merry.

'Different from where?'

'From over there.' Merry nodded across to the far side.

'I always wondered why you chose Lambeth,' said Freddy.

'I didn't. Had I known what a terrible slum it was I would never have gone near it.'

She told him about the evening of the day her parents threw her out of the house. How she had wandered the streets for hours, thinking, not thinking, surely there was a friend she could call on? But no, the only people who came to mind were family acquaintances and it was crucial, above all else it was crucial to break off all family ties, that was the one thing she was certain of. And somehow her wanderings had taken her over the river, to Salamanca

Road, quite by chance.

'You would never have met the magnificent Mrs Vlatsky,' Freddy observed. 'Who thinks of you as her daughter. It's a wonder, in sense . . .' he paused and turned to look at her. 'How much love you inspire, you of all people.'

She didn't rise to that. 'Tell that to my mother.'

'Your mother knows all too well. Poor mama.'

'You've met her too then?'

'Of course. I make it my business, as I told you. To meddle in your affairs as much as possible without annoying you. Or telling you, which is the same thing.'

She frowned at him. 'Sometimes I believe you speak in code, Freddy Prentice.'

'Unfortunately that is true, and necessary. If we all said what we meant it would be a strange world. What would we do with all the time we saved?'

She had no answer to that so she gave none.

'If you believe, as I do, that things work out for the best if you allow them to, it leads to a very simple life. That's not to say that you don't on occasion have to get off your behind and make things happen. Like knocking on your mama's door.'

'Never.'

'Shame. I could come with you.'

'No, Freddy.'

Freddy sighed and placed an arm around the back of the bench on which they sat. 'You are looking exceptionally beautiful this morning, if you don't mind my saying so,' he said.

Merry flushed and toyed with a stray strand of hair.

'What was it that you wanted to see me about?'

There was a very long pause. Then without looking at him Merry said, 'Freddy will you marry me?' And before he could answer she went on, 'I quite understand if the answer is no, it would not be in the least surprising, or unexpected. But in that case we need never see one another again as I would die of embarrassment and I would not know what to say to you.'

There was another tiny pause before she added, 'Clumsily put, I think.'

Freddy opened his mouth to speak and she said, 'I apologise for taking you by surprise, I didn't know how else to put it, I am tired of . . . tired of . . .'

'Tired of what, my sweet?'

'Waiting for some kind of sign perhaps. I don't know. In the end – I'm not at all sure I would make an ideal wife, in many ways I think I would be an impossible handful. And I do not intend to give up my work, that has to be understood. I don't want – I don't think I want children but I am prepared to be persuaded otherwise. I cannot cook and housework terrifies me. There it is,' she said finally.

In all the time of speaking she did not look at him once. 'Speak to me.'

'If I can get a word in edgeways.' He took hold of her hand and examined it, as if it were a strange and exotic object. 'You know the answer.'

'Do I?'

'I would very much like children,' said Freddy. 'They are the wonders of the world, I believe you would agree if you allowed yourself to. As for working, that goes without saying. If we were to take up the kind offer of Mrs Amanda – and I am including myself in this – I also think there will be glorious opportunities lying ahead of us. Cooking and cleaning and so forth will look after itself one way or another. However I have to warn you I would be fiercely faithful, my heart would never stray. I would have your best interests at heart at all times, although I like to think I would have the wit to make myself scarce if and whenever I thought it necessary. If you think – if you *really* think you could spend your life with such a fellow then the answer is, resoundingly, yes.'

With which he took her face between his hands and kissed her with the utmost tenderness.

~

A week later Virginia Stephenson arrived at her home in St Leonard's Terrace after a shopping trip to find two strangers sitting in her drawing room. Rather, one of them looked vaguely familiar though she couldn't immediately place him. The other, after a long moment of miscomprehension, turned out to be her daughter.

The gentleman rose to his feet as she entered and introduced himself as Freddy Prentice. 'I'm engaged to be married to your daughter,' he said genially, as she took his proffered hand and shook it tentatively. 'We have met before, briefly, there's no reason why you should remember.'

'Oh, at the Academy, yes,' said Virginia vaguely. 'I do remember. We got chatting, yes. How are you?'

'Extremely well, thank you Mrs Stephenson, and I must say I am delighted to meet you in a rather different capacity. We have come' – he turned to glance at Meredith – 'to invite you to our wedding.'

'Oh.' She was having difficulty getting her brain to function fully. This moment, that she had dreamed of so many, many times was not how she imagined it to be. Her first thought was annoyance that it had happened without warning, when she was tired and slightly frazzled after an abortive shopping expedition to Selfridge's department store and she had no time to check her appearance, let alone have a good sit down. And now, not just all that but a wedding, to a man she barely knew and what would Maurice say?

'Congratulations,' she stammered.

Her daughter was watching her from her chair, from which she was making no attempt to rise.

'Hello Meredith,' said Meredith's mother. So formal, how ridiculous. 'How lovely to see you again.'

The two women continued to stare at one another almost as if they had never met. Freddy looked from one to another with amusement.

'She didn't want to come,' he addressed Meredith's mother. 'It's been a long time I understand, and there's been an estrangement. She told me she was waiting for you to visit her and I told her you had done so, more than once I believe, and, well, if each is waiting for the other to make the first move we could all die in the waiting.' He laughed. Mrs Stephenson smiled weakly. 'She will be a handful, she has told me already, I'm quite prepared, or I hope I am. But I may need your assistance or your advice on occasion.' He smiled disarmingly at Meredith's mother.

Virginia sank slowly into an armchair. 'It's rather a lot to take in,' she said. 'I'm sorry if I appear . . .' she fussed with her hair for a moment. 'I've been waiting for this moment for a long time. And now that it's here . . .' she stopped, and looked at her daughter, and to her shock and shame she began to cry.

'I'm sorry to spring it on you like this.' Freddy offered his handkerchief, which she refused. 'It is clean. But I thought, or Merry thought if we wrote first that you might not agree to see us. Sneaky in a way I suppose, but there it is.'

'Not agree to see you! How could you think that? Oh Meredith!' She got to her feet and sank onto her knees in front of her daughter. Meredith remained where she was, unmoving and apparently unmoved. 'Why do you think I came to visit you all those times? Why do you think I saw every play you were in, wherever I could find you? And to the Academy? Every day . . .' Virginia took hold of her daughter's hands and pumped them up and down in agitation. 'I think about you every day. Oh, gracious me.'

She let go of her daughter's hands and got swiftly to her feet. 'I am so sorry,' she said to Freddy. 'I quite forgot myself.' She sniffed into her handkerchief and laughed with embarrassment and regained her seat and her composure.

'Fred darling,' said Meredith. 'Would you mind leaving us alone for a moment?'

'Not in the least,' said Freddy. 'I will wait . . .' he gestured vaguely beyond the door. And with a bow first to Mrs Stephenson and then to her daughter, he backed out of the room.

He was not intentionally eavesdropping, but having found himself in the hallway of an unfamiliar house to which he had not been invited there was little he could do but lurk right there in the hallway close to the drawing room door, through which he could not avoid listening.

At first it was quiet, totally quiet. Then he could hear low murmuring and the odd raised voice – Merry's – followed by more low murmuring and more silence. This continued for some time, maybe ten minutes or more. Meanwhile Freddy studied a picture on the wall of of a man in military uniform, perhaps Meredith's father, or more likely *his* father – Freddy wasn't particularly up on the history of military uniforms – and he mildly contemplated what Merry's father might make of him; or more to the point, what he might make of Freddy's father. Meanwhile he pondered on what he would find to say for himself should anyone appear to challenge his presence there in the hallway. He knew the master of the house was out (though it didn't mean he may not come home at any moment, and *then* what would Freddy have to say for himself?), but he also knew how servants gossip, and how the absence of the Stephensons' only offspring must have been a prime topic of conversation over the years 'downstairs'.

More raised voices, this time Merry's and her mother's. Freddy shivered, and idly examined himself in the hallway mirror.

To have gone from the opulence of this five-storey terraced elegance to the two-storey run-down hovel – as Freddy saw it – in Lambeth would have taken some doing on Merry's part. She claimed she grew to find Lambeth altogether friendlier and more homely, and he could understand that. Brought up in relative poverty as he was – though you'd never know it from his demeanour, such is the skill of the actor – Freddy found affluence and its trimmings, servants especially, both intriguing and intimidating.

He looked at his watch. Twenty minutes had passed. More murmurings, and then something quite unexpected: a laugh. Merry's initially, and then her mother's. Freddy drew a deep breath. His huge, generous heart was swelling. Moments later the door to the drawing room opened and Merry emerged, followed closely by her mother. He could see from their shining eyes – how alike they were – they had been crying, both of them. And he wanted to cry too. As Merry threw herself into his arms (a first) he instinctively reached out a hand to her mother and she shyly approached and allowed him to place his arms around the two of them. And there they stood, for some time, the three of them, clutched in a wordless embrace.

Epilogue

It was, predictably, a relatively stormy marriage. In the first six months Merry walked out of the marital home no fewer than three times: the first to her old place in Lambeth (where to her annoyance she learned her room had at last been let out, as Mrs Vlatsky sorrowfully explained) and then to the family home in Chelsea, the door to which was now permanently open. Brigadier Stephenson's views on the whole matter were not recorded, but it is believed his wife had taken it upon herself to make their domestic decisions. Her new confidence was put down, according to friends, to her involvement with the suffragette movement and in particular to her brief spell in Holloway Prison as a result of being in the wrong place at the wrong time (or the right place at the right time, depending on how you view these things), which in turn had opened her eyes to a world she had hitherto known nothing about.

This political commitment, while frowned on by her husband and many of her friends, though not all (Antonia was an obvious exception), brought Virginia and her daughter oddly closer together. While Merry never did quite espouse the notion of female suffrage she did admire her mother's spirit and courage and sacrifice, more than she would care to admit. For her part, Mrs Stephenson became Merry's biggest champion in her new venture as Principal of the Prentice Academy for Young Women, based in Camden Town.

In time things settled down. As Merry became more and more absorbed in her new role as teacher and mentor to her young pupils, her husband alongside her, so she learned the wisdom of calm reflection. Of thinking before acting. She was a role model now, with responsibilities to a dozen or more impressionable young women who looked up to her, who to a lesser or greater extent worshipped her, as young Miranda had once done. Miranda, who now worked as an assistant to Merry and Freddy, a position she initiated and filled with great efficiency and self-effacement.

Moreover she had learned the true meaning of requited love. Like so many woman down the ages Merry had always inclined towards the unavailable, or at least the unpredictable. To know that there was someone at her side at all times, no matter what, unfazed by her whims and moods – even, dare one say it, amused by them – was not something she found easy to come to terms with. But time and maturity made her see things rather differently.

Moreover that the girls of the Academy were, as a group, head over heels in love with the Principal's husband was a fact not lost on the Principal herself, and was perhaps one of the reasons Merry decided not just to remain in the marital home for the foreseeable in order to keep a close eye on things, but to relish her new position as matriarch. With the arrival a year later of their first child, a boy they named Harley (after Freddy's hero Harley Granville Barker; Merry, not quite seriously, wanted to name him Nicholai, at which point Freddy, not quite seriously, threatened to walk out of the house and never return), something rather radical happened to

Merry's world view. Her ambitions and her priorities disappeared in the pools of the little creature's dark eyes and nothing, but nothing would thwart her insistence on taking time off work to nurture and wean the infant. This child was going to grow up surrounded by love and attention from her working father and mother. All things were possible.

Mrs Vlatsky joined the list of the Academy's supporters, who included of course Mrs Amanda and her husband and a number of other endlessly generous benefactors, some of whom were anonymous. This last group included Mrs Maurice Stephenson, who unknown to both her daughter and her husband had taken it upon herself to secretly raise funds from her own well-heeled friends, the Gullivers in particular – 'So much money they don't know what to do with it'. Mrs V was not a benefactor, but as far as enthusiasm and support were concerned she was, as Merry described her, 'the star of the show'.

The Academy was not in any way a drama school, nor did it pretend to be. Its object, its mission, was to prepare young women from all backgrounds for life in the twentieth century where they would be expected not just to work for a living but to find fulfilment outside the home as well as within it. It was a broad brief, you could say, and academic tuition played a relatively small part in it on the understanding that the girls had already served that particular sentence. The focus was on *character*, as Merry described it, and *aspiration*. To this end she and Freddy called on their actor friends to run the odd class on improvisation, Shakespeare, speech and movement and, at Freddy's insistence, the history of theatre with a special emphasis on Ibsen, Shaw and the life and works of Harley Granville Barker. For her part Merry lectured on and demonstrated the theatrical System as created by the great Russian actor and director Konstantin Stanislavsky. It was hardly surprising therefore that several of the Academy's students left with ambitions to become professional actors, and on Merry's suggestion to audition for ADA, the institution that had, in her view, so mistakenly snubbed her all those years ago.

Merry even invited her old friend Gaye Worth (Tilling) to talk to the girls about her experiences in music hall and understudying and appearing in *The Merry Widow*. She taught them a bawdy song which they learned with great gusto. At Freddy's suggestion they arranged an outing to a music hall in East London and trips to see Shakespeare and J M Barrie in the West End and Shaw and Galsworthy at the Court. From time to time a nervous parent reached out a restraining hand to remind this theatrical couple to pull in the reins somewhat. But otherwise the Academy went from strength to strength, and in time they managed to raise the funds to offer scholarships to girls from humbler backgrounds.

But then the inevitable happened.

It is said once an actor always an actor. That if ever one has stood on a stage and held a thousand people in the palm of one's hand no other experience can come close, which is why so many actors and actresses keep going even when the odds are obviously not in their favour. Call it an addiction or a drug, once it gets its claws into you the acting habit is hard to shake off.

Both Merry and Freddy had received offers of acting engagements from time to time – ironical, from Merry's point of view, that they should appear only when she was not available – but none of them were so enticing they could not turn them down without regret.

However when the opportunity arose to play Rosalind

in Shakespeare's *As You Like It* at the Garrick Theatre in the West End Merry could not say no.

'I always wanted to play Rosalind,' she told Freddy. 'And it's only for eight weeks, you can manage without me for eight weeks, surely.'

It wasn't the eight weeks that concerned Freddy, it was the possibility that this was the thin end of the wedge, that the acting demon would latch onto Merry and not let go. Nonetheless there was no stopping Merry when, as her husband described it, her 'tail was up.'

That she was Rosalind to the manner born was a fact that Merry had known all her working life. She had the height and the natural wit, the charm and presence to play a spirited woman who spends most of the play dressed as a man 'flirting' with her lover. It was as if the part were written for her.

As a youngster she had dismissed Shakespeare's comedies, especially those featuring cross-dressing, as far-fetched. The audience, she declared, could never be fooled by a woman dressed as a man. But children can be very literal-minded; what Merry did not yet have the maturity to appreciate was what is commonly called 'the magic of theatre', where under the spell of a company of actors an audience is prepared to suspend their disbelief and allow themselves to be transported into a world of make-believe and fairy tale. Shakespeare understood this like no other. Scholars had written endlessly tedious treatises about it. It was something every actor and actress understood, how else could they perform any role with conviction?

Meredith's performance was generally lauded by the critics, some of whom exclaimed in rapture 'Where has this miraculous creature come from? Why have we not seen her before?' which Merry found both gratifying and amusingly mystifying.

But then some way into the run an odd thing happened. In the middle of a scene in the Forest of Arden, Merry as Rosalind dressed as a young man called Ganymede lent back casually against a prop tree and felt it wobble. Suppressing a giggle she continued with the scene but as she gazed into the eyes of her Orsino all she could think of was 'This is silly'.

The magic had disappeared. She felt suddenly ridiculous. She badly wanted to laugh out loud. The whole stage setting with its wobbly trees and painted backdrop looked simply ludicrous. She was far too old and worldly-wise to be playing let's pretend in front of an audience of supposed grownups. It was child's work, child's play perhaps, she wanted none of it.

To cap it all, nobody noticed, except her Orsino of course, who rather imagined she'd had a minor breakdown. 'The look on your face!' he exclaimed later, with a laugh.

'What did you see?'

'Horror, disgust, disdain, as if someone had presented you with a plate of bad meat. Your lip literally curled, I didn't think such a thing was truly possible.'

'Indigestion,' she said.

'Yes, that's what I rather thought. Best not to eat before a performance I think.'

She completed the run and nobody remarked on the change in her performance, which made it all the more nonsensical.

'Whatever is the opposite of transported,' she told Freddy, 'that is what I was. It was like a veil lifting, everything was suddenly razor-sharp, and rational, like seeing the light for the first time. And that was it, I couldn't get it back, I couldn't find the magic again.' She felt she ought to be sad, even tearful, but the thought of it simply made her laugh.

Freddy stroked her cheek and tried to hide his relief.

'You're not in the least sorry for me, are you Fred?'

'I am not,' said Freddy.

'I'm not sure I shall ever be able to step on a stage again,' she said, with a melodramatic sigh.

'Thank God for that,' said Freddy.

'But it's all I ever wanted to do. It was my driving force, the reason I got up In the morning, the reason I left home, everything. It makes no sense at all.'

'It makes perfect sense,' said her husband. 'Welcome back to reality, Mrs Prentice.'

If you enjoyed this book and you could post a review on the platform you bought it from you would make this author very happy.

~

If you would like a FREE copy of my short story YOUNG CLAUDIA please subscribe to my occasional newsletter at https://patsytrench.com. You can opt out at any time.

Author biography

Patsy Trench has spent her life working in the theatre. She was an actress for twenty years in theatre and television in the UK and Australia. She has written scripts for stage and (TV) screen and co-founded *The Children's Musical Theatre of London,* creating original musicals with primary school children. She began writing books later in life and so far is the author of three non fiction books about colonial Australia based on her own family history and five novels about women bucking tradition in the recent past. When she is not writing books she teaches theatre part-time and organises theatre trips for overseas students. In her free time she fossicks for ancient treasure on the Thames foreshore, crochets, rag rugs, babysits and discovers new and fascinating snippets of history of her native city.

She lives in London. She has two adult offspring and one grandson.

Social media links:

Website: https://patsytrench.com/
Facebook: PatsyTrenchWriting
Twitter (X): @PatsyTrench
Instagram: PatsyTrenchAuthor
Substack: patsytrenchauthor@substack.com